SHORT AND SHORTER STORIES

DOUG INGOLD

Wolfenden

Copyright © 2023 by Douglas A. Ingold

ISBN (print) 978-0-9973513-4-7
ISBN (eBook) 978-0-9973513-5-4

Library of Congress Control Number: 2023902543

Published by

Wolfenden

Wolfenden Publishers
Arcata, California
Contact: wlfndn3@gmail.com

Cover, layout and design by
Robert Stedman Pte Ltd, Singapore

Printed in the USA

Novels by

Doug Ingold

There Came a Contagion

Rosyland: A Novel in III Acts

Square

The Henderson Memories

In the Big City

This book is dedicated to fiction lovers
Thanks once again to **NINA** whose writing and editing skills, love, patience, tolerance and careful eyes have been invaluable over the several decades these stories were written.
And to **BONNIE BURGESS** for her excellent proofreading; thus leaving to me full responsibility for any errors and clunkers found within.

SHORT AND SHORTER STORIES

CONTENTS

INTRODUCTION

For a few of us, stories are more real than facts, certainly more interesting, and possibly more true. Elena Ferrante uses the term "literary truth" to describe the "truth" that can emerge unstated and unbidden from a novel or story.

Much of my life, it seems, I have spent reading and writing fiction, or if not writing, then forcing stories back into the recesses of my mind so I could accomplish more practical tasks. In my mid-thirties, I organized my time in such a way that I could write for a few hours every week. Some of the stories in this book were born in those years.

Over the next fifty years I completed and self-published five novels, wrote a stage play and two screenplays, started several aborted novels, completed a few poems and short stories. From this debris I have selected for this slender volume ten short stories and six snips of "flash-fiction."

WEIGHT OF THE DOG and INDEPENDENT STUDY were published decades ago in small magazines. A few of the "flash" pieces have been printed in the North Coast Journal. The remaining stories are making their initial public appearance.

I make no claim that you will discover any truth here, but I do hope you will find some pleasure.

Doug Ingold
Arcata, California

BREAKFAST

Elaine's thirteen-year-old daughter carries a knife hidden in her clothing. Elaine knows this. She's been threatened with the tip of the quavering six-inch blade pointed toward her throat, the handle wrapped in black plastic tape. Where will it be hidden this morning? Inside the boot against her daughter's left calf, flat across the small of her back, up the sleeve of the familiar denim jacket? But when Elaine turns from the stove to look, all she sees approaching the table is her child, skinny, scared, too young. "You want some bacon with your eggs, hon?"

WEIGHT OF THE DOG

I'm out in the garage putting away the lawnmower when I hear the dog hit the water. This is a Saturday afternoon about two-thirty. I got a backyard full of guests about to arrive. I got a wife complaining there's a million things to do and why am I mowing the lawn at the last minute when it doesn't need mowing all that bad anyway. And now I leave the gate open five minutes and I got this dog in the pool.

I grab a horseshoe from the set on the wall. I'm yelling as I run out the garage. I make the corner flat out and I'm angling for the right side of the pool. My left arm is bent back, the horseshoe poised to throw.

It's Willow again, the Anderson's Irish setter. She's swimming toward me happy as a seal. Her reddish-brown hair is flowing out, her dumb face gleeful with victory. I watch the alarm slowly register as she turns in mid-stroke and makes for the far edge. I heave the horseshoe and I have this fine short sensation of terror and rage skillfully concocted and flowing like mercury out along my arm and into the force of the throw.

That's when I remember the clothesline. We got a drier, but Connie loves the smell of clothes off a line so she had me rig one up last week between the garage and the diving platform. Taking it down was one of the things Connie said had to be done before the guests arrived, one of the things more pressing than mowing the lawn.

The clothesline takes me down. It catches me across the chest at the full thrust of my follow through. It curls me into a back flip and drops me like a ripe grape at the edge of the concrete. Meanwhile the horseshoe connects with the base of Willow's neck just above the waterline. She might survive if someone pulls her from the water, but the only witnesses are Connie—who hearing my yell has turned toward the back door—and Charles and Mindy Cross—the first guests, stepping around the corner of the house to find me swirling in mid-air—and everybody's too enchanted by the gymnastics to notice an unconscious animal slowing sinking in the pool.

§

"But I did mean to kill her," I'm saying to Connie. This is six hours later. At her insistence I'm sitting in bed propped up against the pillows. "I hated that dog... well, maybe I didn't mean to kill her—I don't know."

"Anyway, that's what you said to the Crosses. 'But I didn't mean to kill her.' It was a confession, Harry, anyway you look at it."

I'm climbing out of the bed and going to the window. The dog is lying against the fence, a rusty mound. The hair along her back has dried and tufts rise now and then in the evening breeze.

Connie comes over. She stands on the tips of her toes and presses her forehead against the window. "You can't see it from here but the horseshoe is still down there. Bright red at the bottom of the pool." She seems pleased by the thought of it. As if I had created something aesthetically pure.

"Big dog," I say.

"I'm thinking about the children," she adds after a moment. "The Anderson kids. They were crazy about that dog."

"That dog was a communal nightmare." I'm tapping the window frame with the heel of my fist. "She ran all over the neighborhood. She stormed through pools and flowerbeds. She cleaned out every available cat dish in a six-block area and still made it home in time for dinner." I feel Connie watching me and stop beating on the woodwork. "The man's a cop. You expect more responsibility from a man like that."

"It's the kids I'm thinking about," Connie says again.

"The first time I talked to Anderson about it, what'd he say? 'It's the kids' dog,' he said. 'Wouldn't hurt a flea.' 'So, who's talking about fleas?' that's what I should have said. Another time he said to me, 'The dog loves water, that's just the way she is.' Jesus."

Connie sighs. She's heard it all before. "It's getting dark, they'll start to wonder."

"Hey, what I should do is drag that dog over there and throw her on the porch. What I should do is tell Anderson to his face that the next time he gets a dog for his kids he should take some responsibility for it. That's what I should do."

"Lie down, Harry," Connie says. She's leading me back to the bed. Her fingers begin to move along my back. She's good at this sort of thing, Connie is. "Relax, Harry," she says, "just relax."

§

It's dark now and I'm outside by the pool. There are crickets and from open windows the last clatter of dishes being put away. A lot of nights I'm out here alone, the yard lights off, numbers streaming through my head. "Yes, but that's if everything goes right," I say to myself, "but things don't go right."

The Andersons live out of the cul-de-sac and down the street a couple of doors. No way to tell from where I'm sitting if they're home. But for the dog I wouldn't have the pleasure. Connie's acquainted with the kids from school. Nice enough kids, she says. Sometimes

Anderson parks the patrol car in the driveway. People say it adds to the security of the neighborhood.

Don't be a fool, Harry, I'm thinking. Thing to do is get the dog out of the yard and you out of the mess. It doesn't take a mainframe to see there's no forgiveness in that man. He bites off his sentences like nails. He feeds on getting even.

The smell of charcoal lingers, the crisp edges of fat from the steaks. I was standing there twisted through the back cooking each one to order, dog drying, people sweating. It's ninety degrees and no one is going in the pool. Dead-dog memory is like a screen between them and the water. No one playing horseshoes either. I lean forward; the horseshoe is no longer visible.

Now I'm at the fence, kneeling down beside the evidence. Anderson or no Anderson I got regrets. The dog loved water. I could've chased her out one more time. I give a gentle tug on a foreleg. It's beginning to stiffen. I'm dragging the body of the dog through the new-mown grass of the backyard, trying not to aggravate the back. "Rash," I'm saying.

It's a heavy lift into the trunk. The rear legs want to jut out and I have to shove them down into the corner. The shovel's too long, has to be pried in. Like pillboxes these cars. My dad drove the old 98's. You could camp in those trunks.

Street lights are everywhere up and down the neighborhood. At the Anderson's house the lights are on. The honest thing would be to knock on the front door, but I drive by. Anderson wouldn't be tormented by this sort of thing if circumstances were reversed. He'd be gloating. What a throw, he'd be saying to his cop buddies.

I'm turning at the corner. I'm driving slowly up Hillcrest toward the small park at the top. "Could drop her anywhere," I'm thinking. "Look like a car got her." It's hard telling though who might be sitting out on a night like this. Neighborhood Watch Area. Signs are all over the place. The retirees have nothing to do but watch for suspicious conduct.

"But I'm not the crook. If there's criminal behavior here it's Anderson not me."

I skirt the park slowly. There are lights all through it illuminating the paths. Joggers. People walk here after dark. I drop back down and turn out of the subdivision onto McNeil Avenue in sporadic traffic.

My reception's spiffy tonight. I'm getting a golden age picture of the Anderson home. The kids are badgering their parents to go out in the car looking. "Something's happened to her, Mom, I know it!" This is around a large oblong dining room table. The mother dusting with a cloth is wearing a print dress and an apron. The kids have freckles in black and white.

I turn right onto Route 78, four lanes; traffic moving nicely south toward Windsor. There will be about seven or eight miles of farmland along here and the road runs parallel to a stream. I'm nearing the junction with Airport Road when a red light flashes in the rearview mirror. It's right behind me and the officer is using a spotlight to pull me over.

You make your money with money and you're always running the numbers: I drive over twenty thousand miles a year and I haven't been stopped in three years—illegal right-hand turn, a picky call by a nervous rookie. This trip is no more than twenty miles—no, you could only count the way out—ten miles. One in six thousand. Convey these facts to an astrologer and she'd tell you to get in bed and belt a pillow over your head.

The highway patrolman, a man with full lips and smooth skin, takes my license back to the car to run a check. They do it by the book anymore, too many crazies on the road. He returns and hands over my license.

"Sir, you have no taillights. Were you aware of that?"

No, I was not aware of that. The officer opens the door and together we lean under the dash to examine the fuses. The officer smells strongly of cologne. The fuses are fine.

"Must be a loose wire," the officer says. He's being kind enough, trying to help. "Have you been in the trunk lately? Sometimes you can jar a wire loose and not know it."

I'm sitting very still for a moment. Cars are passing at what seem like breakneck speeds. I feel their sounds enter and pass through me unimpeded as though I am air. Suddenly, I'm flinging open the door, nearly knocking the policeman off his feet.

"Officer, I think you've got it! Look at this." I lead him to the back of the car and open the trunk. Willow's oily dead eye gleams out eerily, catching the lights of the passing cars.

We're silent awhile, as if in contemplation. Then I say, "I found her on the street in front of the house. Wife knows the kids. Bad family. We thought it would be better if they didn't know."

The officer seems genuinely moved. He helps me locate the wire and then allows me to resume my journey. I'm pulling away, feeling better than I have all day. In the rush of successful deception my back has spawned new and resilient fibers, my chest is balmed by its own juices.

But then later, on a small flat by the stream working with the shovel at the edge of the headlight beams, I'm thinking, What a fool to throw in that gratuitous remark about a bad family. All these cops must know one another. Anderson mentions the missing dog and the officer remembers the contents of the trunk. "He had my license, Con," I'm muttering. "Ran a make on our car." "Why do they call it, 'Run a make on a car?'" That's just the kind of thing Connie would ask and I have no idea. Television dribble.

I'm wishing I'd worn something with heavy soles. I've pulled Willow from the car and laid her beside the grave, a measure for the eye. Occasions for mourning. I'm a kid giving ritual to the burial of worms, baby birds. Just what I'm now denying the Anderson kids.

I'm sweating and the back throbs. The dry stony earth seems determined to resist my desires. It has no appetite for swallowing a dead dog or covering a crime. "Really no reason to bury her. I could have just left her there," I'm saying, as though it were over and I'm home with Connie's fingers working my back. "It matters to no one, least of all to the dog." The breeze has died and dew is settling on the grass. I'm still digging. I enjoy the smell of the earth. I should have been a gardener.

§

Job finished, coast clear. I stop at a franchise, order a Denver sandwich and a cup of coffee. In the restroom I wash my hands up past the wrists. Much too soon for there to be any smell. I'm imagining it.

Just as my order arrives two cops walk into the restaurant and sit down at the counter. Anderson does not recognize me or hear my mind running through the rough calculations: number of restaurants in town, the amount of time in any month Anderson and I might spend in them…. "You know, Con," I'm thinking a few minutes later, "Willow might become a legend among the Anderson children. Every Irish setter will cause a little stir. Against all reason they will continue to look for her. Their mourning will be spread and thus thinned. Her very absence will sustain them."

There's a mirror behind the counter so I'm cautious in my observation. Anderson's getting heavy in the jowls and midsection. The tailored sky-blue shirt is too taut across his back. A thickness, I'm thinking, born of leaning his exasperation on others.

I'm finishing my sandwich, I'm picking up my check. I'm starting for the cash register. Beyond that, the door. I'm acquitted and refreshed. I've dusted a little irritant around his living room: "You're a cop, why can't you find our dog?"

Then I'm stopping at his back. Watching in the mirror, I see recognition come up on my neighbor's face.

"Anderson," I say, "there's some things I want to tell you."

"Yeah?" Anderson's not interested. He has his liver and onions to attend to, his soggy cloud of mashed potatoes, his peas greener than the lawn I mowed so long ago this morning.

When the words start coming out they're like sparks flying off a sharpening stone. There's no effort. The stone's spinning fast. I just have to touch down, touch gently down the edged steel and the words shoot out like sparks.

INDEPENDENT STUDY

When Karen mentioned the pistol, her mother went through the roof. "Through the roof," Karen thought, was exactly how her mother would have described it had it been someone other than herself who went. At the moment, though, she was more interested in labeling Karen's behavior than her own. "Irresponsible," "Foolish" and "Quite possibly illegal," were among the terms used. She went on to predict that Karen's father would be furious and she recommended that Karen "turn right around" and take the pistol back to the sporting goods store where she bought it.

Karen moved the receiver from one ear to the other and stretched out her long legs. She was sitting on the living room carpet with her back against the wall. In September the serviceman had left the telephone on the floor after connecting it to the jack and three months later it was still there.

"Just last month," she finally said, interrupting her mother's ongoing prophesy of doom, "an apartment right across the street was broken into. And two weeks ago the liquor store on the corner was robbed at gun point. At gun point, Mom. I'm just trying to protect myself, that's all." She stretched the phone cord toward the tip of her nose, glared along the coils and let them snap away.

"You'll kill yourself, that's what you'll do." The tone suggested that Karen's death was not only certain to occur, but soon, and would most likely be self-inflicted.

"Eddie knows all about guns, Mother. He has promised to teach me everything I need to know before we even load it." And before her mother could say something derogatory about Eddie she added, "And Dad has kept at least two guns in the bedroom closet ever since I can remember."

"That's not the same and you know it. Those are hunting guns, and your father is not…well…isn't it illegal for Eddie to have a gun?"

"The gun is mine, Mother. There's nothing illegal about *my* having a gun."

"Your father will know about that."

"Right," Karen said, and hung up the phone.

In the kitchen she lifted the lid from the maroon box and stared down at the pistol. The man at the store had assured her it was not loaded and perfectly safe. He had worked the mechanism with careless ease while explaining that this particular model, a best seller, made an ideal bedside weapon. Given a few hours' practice, he said, she would be using it as effectively as any man.

Karen ran a finger across the scored plastic grip and then along the cold metal of the barrel. Snuggled in its velvety casing, the weapon seemed as innocent and as harmless as the clarinet she had played through high school. Still, she could not bring herself to pick it up. She replaced the lid and carried the surprisingly heavy box back to the bedroom closet.

§

Eddie could not buy the pistol himself because he was on probation. Karen thought the restriction was ridiculous because Eddie's "crime" had nothing to do with guns. He had been involved in an automobile accident in which the other driver had been injured. The whole thing happened before she met him but Eddie told her all about it after they started going together. He had drunk only one beer, he said, but the police found an open container in his car and he was convicted of drunk driving. The judge suspended his driver's license for a year.

"But that's not fair, one beer?" Karen said when he explained it to her. "Can't you appeal?"

"Rich people appeal," Eddie said. "The rest of us wait it out."

Karen poured some salt on the restaurant table and drew a line through it. "So that's why you never drive," she said. "That night at the party you said it was because you'd just sold your car."

"I had just sold it. But that's why. It was creamed and all I had was liability. That old man pulled right out in front of me. You know how they are. They grew up with horses and buggies. What can you expect?"

Karen made a cross in the salt and drew a circle around it. Her father was a claims adjuster. He knew a lot of attorneys. Maybe he would have a suggestion.

"I'd just met you that night," Eddie added after a moment.

"Oh, I understand. There's no reason you should have told me the whole story." She looked up from her drawing and smiled.

§

She was standing in front of the apartment waiting for the bus to campus when Eddie and his friend James came home from work. James parked the old Impala across the street and Eddie got out with a six-pack in each hand. He had graduated from high school three years before but he still wore his orange and black letter-jacket with the football sewn on the chest. He stopped on the curb and looked at her with his cocky smile.

"Hey, lady," he yelled across the street, "burn your mouth lately? We got pizza."

Karen giggled. "Sorry, I don't talk to strangers."

"James, show the lady the pizza. Sausage, mushrooms, extra tomatoes."

"I have to go to class," she said wincing.

Eddie crossed the street, grinning, using his jaunty walk. He put his arms around her, the cans clanking against her back. "Sausage," he repeated slowly, looking down into her eyes. "Mushrooms. Lots and lots of tomatoes. Cheese that'll stretch from your toes to your lovely lips." He kissed her.

The bus was coming. "Eddie, I have to go. Really, I have to."

"Sausage," he whispered in her ear. "Mushrooms. Acres and acres of tomatoes."

"I'll end up like Maureen if I don't go."

"Jesus." He dropped his arms and released her. "Say, did you get it?"

"Look in the closet," she shouted from the door of the bus.

Before Eddie, Karen had shared the apartment with Maureen. They had been best friends in high school and together they had moved from Modesto to Santa Rosa to attend college. But while Karen found classwork exciting, Maureen became quickly spellbound by social activities: everything from bridge games at ten in the morning to keg parties through the night. She dropped out of school after spending five days in bed existing on Uneeda biscuits and quarts of milk, paralyzed between her fear of her teachers if she returned to class and of her parents if she went home. It was during those five days—while Karen was devoting hours to cajoling and pleading with Maureen—that Eddie told her he was looking for a place to live. He would take Maureen's room—assuming Maureen ever got out of the bed—and they would share the rent and utilities. That arrangement lasted two and a half nights.

The only problem with Eddie, so far as Karen was concerned, was James who followed Eddie like a scruffy shadow. He spent most of his free time at their apartment. He drank their beer, ate the food Karen prepared, used her towels and left her albums lying around on the floor. At a party in November he broke her full-length mirror while demonstrating his skill at slam dancing.

"He's driving me nuts," she told Eddie when they were in bed after the party.

"He'll pay for the mirror."

"He's creepy."

"He's our wheels, Karen. I got to get to work and back."

"Isn't there a bus? I take a bus."

Eddie grunted. "It's just till I get my license back, babe. If you had a car, or if I had the money to buy you one, I'd put him out now." He turned out the light and stroked her cheek with the tips of his fingers. "He's been my friend for a long time, but he's not going to come between us, Karen, believe me."

The morning following the party Karen called her father and asked if he would buy her a car. Her father said he would like to buy her a car. He said he would if he could afford it and he thought he might be able to next year if she kept her grades up. But as Karen listened to her father she knew he did not want to buy her a car. He wanted her to move back to Modesto and commute to the junior college. "If you were living at home," he said, "I could afford to buy you a car."

§

When Karen returned from class Eddie and James were in the living room drinking beer and "dry shooting" the pistol. She heard a sharp click as she opened the door. The pistol was aimed at her head.

"It's beautiful, babe," Eddie said. "Just the one we talked about. Where'd you put the shells?"

"You didn't say I should buy shells." Karen dropped her pack on the floor and sat down beside him. "I wish you wouldn't aim that at me."

James chuckled, his lips tight across his broken incisor. "It can hardly hurt you, Karen, seeing's how you didn't get any bullets."

Eddie lifted the pistol above his head and slowly lowered it until the short barrel pointed at the volume control of the sound system. "She's right, James. I shouldn't point it at her and I didn't tell her to pick up any shells." The pistol clicked, U2 continued on without pause. "But we're going to need ammo, babe, if I'm going to teach you how to use this little jewel. And that's the important thing. I want you to feel comfortable."

"I should have bought some," Karen admitted. The clerk had tried to sell her some ammunition but at that moment, just buying the pistol had been enough.

Eddie handed Karen his beer and pointed toward the remaining slice of cold pizza. "Your dad called. He said to call him back whenever you got in."

Karen, who did not care much for beer, took a long swallow.

Her father answered the phone on its first ring. "Karen?" he said.

"Yes, Dad."

"Are you all right?"

"Sure, Dad."

"Good, that's good. You sound good." He chuckled. "Have you heard the one about the two drunks in a skyscraper?"

Karen had, but she listened anyway. "That's funny, Dad," she said when he finished.

"How's school? Finals coming up?"

"I'm fine, Dad."

"Good, I'm sure you are." He paused and Karen pictured her mother standing beside him, nudging his broad back the way she did when she wanted him to do something he would rather not do. "Mommy is a little disturbed about what you told her this afternoon." Another pause. "And so am I. Yes, so am I. We're having a hard time understanding why you would buy this pistol without discussing it with us beforehand."

"It's not safe here, Dad. Didn't Mom tell you? The place right across…."

"I'm sure you're concerned, very reasonably concerned, and so are we. But what's most disturbing is why you would do something like this without talking to us first. Frankly, it's similar to the way you allowed Eddie to move into the apartment without consulting with us beforehand. No sooner had we learned about Maureen moving out that we hear that Eddie is already living there. After the fact. Both times after the fact."

She had intended to tell them about Eddie, but as soon as Maureen got home she confessed everything to her parents who promptly telephoned Karen's parents. Maureen found confessing so satisfying she had done it for both of them.

"Daddy, I told Mother…."

"I realize you are a young adult woman, but that doesn't mean we can't worry about you."

"And we still pay the bills."

She had been wrong about her mother standing behind her father. Her mother was on the extension.

"That's not why we're concerned, Lois. Money is not the issue here." Karen could hear her father take a deep breath. "Maybe the thing to do is to get you an apartment in another part of town."

"One without Eddie, perhaps?" Karen said.

"We're not talking about Eddie, Karen," her father told her.

"Maybe we should talk about Eddie," her mother said. "He's at the root of all this."

"Lois."

"I knew you were going to say that, Mother! I just knew it."

"Karen."

"You've got no right to spend your father's hard-earned money on pistols. We're not sending you to

24

college so you can become a terrorist or some other kind of criminal."

"Lois, my God!"

"What was that all about?" Eddie asked when she finally got off the phone.

"That was about parents," Karen said, stalking into the kitchen.

§

The next Saturday James drove them to a secluded spot on the Russian River. It was a clear, cold day with a stiff breeze blowing across the water. As Karen stepped from the car she saw a raven tuck its wings in midflight and roll, cackling loudly. They found a place out of the wind among some large gray boulders and Eddie removed the pistol from its box. He explained the safety features and how the firing system worked. Then he handed it to her.

"It's okay," he said. "It's empty. Aim at that tree over there and squeeze the trigger."

Karen's heart was beating wildly. She was certain the gun would explode in her hand.

"Good," Eddie said when the pistol clicked. "Your dad should have done this for you a long time ago." He demonstrated how the cartridges fit into the clip and the clip into the handle. "Now watch." He aimed at the tree. The sound slammed back at them from the bank of the river. "Now, you do it."

Karen rubbed her palms against her jeans and then took the pistol in both hands. It felt heavy and alive, as if it were capable of acting of its own volition. She pointed it at the tree, arms extended. After what seemed a very long time she felt the handle kick against her palms and the sound explode around her.

"Do it again," Eddie said, chuckling. "And this time keep your eyes open."

"Yeah, Karen, like this." James was standing with his legs wide apart, his eyes tightly shut, his face averted, his clasped arms waving around in front of him.

"Shut up, James," Eddie said, trying not to laugh. "Try it again, Karen."

Karen shook her head and set the pistol on a rock. "I could if I had to, and I would if he wasn't here," she said, glaring at James.

"You want me to leave, Karen? It's a long walk back to town. Have you thought about that?"

"James, just shut up!" Eddie put his arms around Karen and held her. Then he stepped back and looked at her. "It's all right, babe. You won't need to use it, not so long as I'm around."

They kept the pistol in the top drawer of the nightstand on Eddie's side of the bed. Karen did not want it to be loaded. She thought they should keep the ammunition in a separate drawer where they could reach it if they had to. Eddie disagreed. An empty pistol, he explained, was more dangerous than a loaded one.

"You pull a gun on someone you have to be willing and able to use it. Because if they have one, they're sure going to use it on you." Eddie held the pistol in his open palm as if weighing it. "Let's face it, Karen. If some guy comes through that window—he may be coming after you, but it'll be my life on the line."

"It's my pistol," Karen said, after a short pause.

"But who's going to be holding it when the dude comes through the window?"

Karen pulled a strand of hair from the back of her neck and placed the tip in the corner of her mouth. She imagined the weight of the pistol, the way it had wanted to leap out of her hands when she pulled the trigger.

"You are," she said finally.

"Right. I am."

They stared at one another for a moment and then Eddie tossed the gun the bed and laughed. "We're talking like marrieds, babe. Like old marrieds fighting over what channel to watch. That's not us and we don't need to be like that. Let's do this. We keep the pistol in the top drawer, okay?" He raised his palms toward her. "And that's where it stays: empty in the top drawer. But in the same drawer we keep the loaded clip. How's that?"

"That's fine," Karen said softly. And it was fine except that every night before going to sleep Eddie practiced opening the drawer, jamming the clip in the handle and aiming it at the door or window. One night she woke to find him gone and the drawer open. She lay scarcely breathing until he returned to the room. "I thought I heard something," he said, removing the clip.

§

As finals neared Karen spent less time at the apartment. She found she could no longer study there. Either Eddie and James were watching television, or they were drinking beer, talking and laughing, or they were gone, which made her wonder where they were.

On the evening before her first final exam she stayed on campus until the library closed at eleven. When she got back, the apartment was dark and she was alone. She made herself some tea and toast and got into bed with her notebook. On the first day of class her instructor had written a long and complicated definition of sociology on the board and she had carefully copied it down word for word. At the library she had read through all her sociology notes and felt she understood everything, but now, sitting on the bed even the definition was beyond her. While she understood each word, when she tried to blend them into a sentence the meaning became vague and confusing.

Her lips moving silently Karen read the sentence a second time and then a third. Finally, she closed the notebook. She took a sip of tea and then slowly opened the top drawer of the nightstand. It was empty, as somehow she knew it would be.

Karen got up. She walked around the apartment turning on all the lights. In the living room she flipped on the TV and sat down on the couch. A news channel was reporting a story about a cat that had become lost in a campground in southern Utah and now three years later had shown up at its owner's house in Manhattan, Kansas. The large woman seated on a couch with a black long-haired cat on her lap said it was a miracle. As the woman talked, the cat slowly turned and looked toward the camera. Its eyes were as yellow as a child's plastic raincoat.

"That cat is a fraud!" Karen shouted to the empty room, poking her fist at the TV. "And the fat woman too."

STYX

Among those of us waiting on the river bank one was a drunken woman. The rest of us understood but she was still confused, demanding of each of us: "Where am I? Why am I here?"

We ignored her, as if she wasn't there at all.

Finally the ferryman emerged from the mist poling his raft. He pushed up to the small pier and motioned to us. We crowded on board but the woman hesitated.

"Step on, sister," the ferryman said. "From my raft no one falls off."

How we envied her lingering doubt.

THE ROSE COTTAGE

Carolyne, my partner, added the "e" to the end of her name when she was eleven as part of a long revolt against her parents, and she has stuck with it for more than forty years even though it agitates spell-checkers and confuses most everyone else. "There's an 'e,'" she repeats several times a day, most every day of her life, "on the end."

I created a similar problem for my son. His name is Tyler but I have always called him Ty and now everyone does, including his father. "With a 'y,'" it is my son's fate to say, "and no 'e.'" I never cared for Tyler as a name. It's a family name on his father's side that landed on my son as part of a complex negotiation during the pregnancy, but that part is over and I'm not going to go into it. Mark—that's Ty's father—has been married to Lynn for several years now. They have a daughter named Amanda, who recently turned nine. Together we make up Ty's two-household, crosstown, California family.

The morning my son was to graduate from high school, I woke thinking about a third house, the Rose Cottage, which is where Ty was conceived and born and where we lived for four years before Mark and I broke up and we had to sell. I loved that house. I loved it the minute I walked through the door and I knew I had to have it. I remember standing in the kitchen with Mark and the realtor. There were brochures on the counter, photographs, dimensions, a list of included appliances, but all I could see was the charm and all Mark could see was the price.

"We can't afford this," he whispered to me.

"We're just looking," I whispered back. "Can't we at least look?"

"Why look if we can't possibly buy?"

"Mark, really, you are impossible!"

The realtor was staring at us. She was in her early-fifties and worked out of the realty office in the strip mall, a couple of doors from where Mark had opened his first electronics store. Now that I have reached the age she was then, I can better understand the resignation I saw in her face that afternoon. Here we go, the look said, another set of bickering clients.

Mark looked at her, then he looked at me. Then he buried his hands in the pockets of his jeans as if clutching his pocket change.

The realtor said, "Are we okay?"

And I said, "We're okay."

And she said, "Have you noticed the windows here in the kitchen? These are original leaded panes of beveled glass."

I put my hand on the glass. You could feel the lead seams and the cut of the bevels and when you pushed, the window flexed slightly along the joints.

"Oh my God, leaded windows!"

The realtor wanted to move on, seeing no reason to belabor what she recognized as a lost cause.

"The dining room through there was built on later. Like the bathroom we'll see in a minute. You'll like the bay window in that room and the view you get across the pasture to the headlands and the sea. Blue water view. But more interesting is the living room. Part of the original house, the windows in here have multiple panes as well. Not leaded, of course, but real shutters on the outside that you can close in a storm."

"Real shutters! Mark, did you hear that?"

"I heard it." He was still in the kitchen staring at the price on the brochure.

"With hinges and little fashioners," the realtor added. "Remind me and I'll show you when we go out. It's all very Victorian. A Cape Cod. A Cape Cod built on the Pacific. And it's not a knockoff. This house was built during the Civil War."

"A house in Mendocino built during the Civil War! I didn't know this place had been discovered by the Civil War."

"Maybe the Indians built it," Mark suggested from the kitchen. He had moved to the stove and was turning the gas burners on and off, listening to that little scratching noise you get when the spark is produced. Mark was becoming an embarrassment to me and a puzzle to the realtor. What, she seemed to be asking herself, has happened to that nice young man who opened the electronics store at the other end of the mall?

"Now let me show you the fireplace," she said.

We walked to the fireplace, stopped and gaped. The fireplace was huge. The opening in the hearth was four feet high and five feet wide with a massive mantel and chimney.

"And it's still functional," the realtor said.

"Amazing!" I said. "That is amazing!" I bent down and looked into the blackened, charred interior. It was like a cave and you could smell the ashes. "Look in here, Mark."

"What?"

"Come here. Look how big this is. And it's still functional!"

Mark came over. He stood slouching. "Okay, I'm looking."

"It's big!"

"It's big, all right."

"Santa could actually come down this chimney!" I exclaimed. "I mean really!"

We all stared into the fireplace for a moment as if waiting for Santa to pop down out of the chimney, and then Mark said, "Maybe we could rent it out."

The realtor was delighted to hear a positive suggestion from my husband. "You're right, you are absolutely right. This house would make an excellent vacation rental. With its history and character. You'd get top dollar."

"I was thinking of the fireplace," Mark said.

"Just the fireplace?"

Mark dug his hands deeper into his pockets. "Help make the payments."

"He's joking," I said to the realtor as we were climbing the stairs to have a look at the bedrooms. "Mark is always joking."

§

Of course we had a fight about it later. I accused him of being an inconsiderate asshole and he called me a manipulative bitch. I reminded him that he knew what the asking price was before we got to the house and he denied it. He said he would never have gone there had he known the price. I said, he knew the price but he was thinking I wouldn't like it, and when I fell in love, he turned into a creep.

We never remembered anything the same way, that was definitely part of the problem. Then after the fight we had sex, which was a pattern we had. And before he entered me, he did something he frequently did, especially after a fight: he started kissing my arms and he worked his way down to my hands and he kissed each of my fingers. He made a kind of a game out of it, muttering little nothings to each of the fingers, but I knew what he was doing and he knew that I knew. He wasn't hot to kiss my fingers, he was hot to smell them. He was smelling for spermicide. He wanted to make sure I had prepared the diaphragm and put it in place. Mark Chandler was, and to this day remains, a cautious man.

Later, lying in the moonlit room, he said, "We simply can't afford it. There's no way. We'd be buried in debt forever. Or we'd have to sell this place and then we'd still have a mortgage."

"So?" I said. I was in love. There was no turning back.

"So?"

"Well?" I said.

Mark sat up and stared at me, confused. "I thought we were just looking for a simple place in town where we could stay over a couple nights a week."

"Well, we were, but…"

"You've got to be joking, Aurora. We can't sell this place. This is our home. We built it with our own hands. We put in the garden ourselves. We developed the water system. I wired this house. I set up the hydropower system. I installed the solar panels. This house, this place. This is us, Aurora."

"So?" I said.

"So?"

"Well?" I said.

Mark fell back on the bed and stared up at the ceiling. "Jesus, Aurora. We've finally gotten to the point where we could begin to put away a little money. And now this."

§

I had the photo albums out on the kitchen table by the time Carolyne returned from her morning run. (I used to say "jog" but jogging suggests tennis shoes and gray sweats and a laconic everything-flopping kind of movement that is decidedly *not* Carolyne.) I had several shots of the exterior of the Rose Cottage with its blue shiplap siding, its remarkable redbrick chimney with the brick arch over the top, a chimney that had survived more than a hundred years of California tremors; Ty on his Big Wheel rumbling along on the wooden front walk.

"Look at this," I said when we sat down with our coffees. "This is all jasmine. You stepped out the front door and it was like a perfume parlor. And calla lilies and nasturtiums along here. A big rosemary. And this, this was a rose bush. Actually, it was more like a rose tree with a thick gnarly trunk. That's where the name came from. The Rose Cottage. That rose must have been as old as the house. And I knew, Carolyne, I knew the minute I saw it."

"You were nesting," Carolyne said. She opened the bag of croissants and slid them gently onto the platter.

Carolyne knows nothing about nesting. Her wiring is all wrong for nesting. I bit into a croissant and smiled.

"Well?" she said, looking at me expectantly. Stating a point is never enough for Carolyne. She wants a concession.

I shook my head. "Don't think so. I wasn't pregnant when we bought the place. Besides, Mark wasn't ready yet to have a child. Just getting him to move was trauma enough for the poor man. Ty was born a year and a half later."

"You were seeking a nest, I'm sure of it. Where were you living at the time? In that cabin, right? The 'back-to-the-land' thing?"

"So?"

"Forty acres and a goat. I can't believe how many supposedly rational people I know who went through that phase."

"We never had a goat, Carolyne."

"The point is, you knew you wanted to have a child even then. And being a nature girl, you wanted to have your baby at home. Correct me if I'm wrong."

"It's Saturday, Carolyne. You can holster your weapons."

"And, even Aurora, pioneer woman herself, wasn't ready to birth a child in her mid-thirties in a cabin forty minutes or more from the nearest hospital."

I was happy to hear the phone ring. I took another bite of croissant. Carolyne answered the phone and handed it to me. It was Mark. He and Lynn were inviting us over for barbeque following the ceremony.

"Dave's in town," I said after I hung up. "Mark's brother. Ty's uncle Dave. They sent him an invitation and he showed up last night, unannounced."

"Oh, yes, the mysterious uncle Dave. Younger or older than Mark?"

"Two years younger."

"I should have guessed. Mark has older brother written all over him now that I think about it."

I started flipping through an album. "The first Christmas we had the Rose Cottage, Dave came to visit with Sheridan, his wife, and Cassidy their son. Cassidy was nineteen, twenty months. I loved having that kid around the house. You should have seen the Rose Cottage at Christmas. I swear it was straight out of Dickens."

I was looking for Christmas photos, but then glanced at Carolyne and for an instant I saw myself through her eyes. My God, I thought, I have become one of those people. Those people with albums. I put it down and picked up my coffee.

"Wasn't he sort of the problem child, Dave I mean?"

"Mark used to say he brought a lot of Vietnam back with him. He was in and out of our lives for years. I always liked him, actually. Then he met Sheridan and had Cassidy. He and Sheridan fell in love with the coast that Christmas. I thought it was just a fantasy, you know how when you go on vacation. Mark and I wanted to move to Maui the time we went there."

"That's what got me here," Carolyne admitted.

"Anyway, a couple of months later, Dave shows up. He's going to find work, he says, and Sheridan and Cassidy will join him at the end of the school year. She was a teacher, kindergarten, I think. So, Mark helped Dave get a job driving a fork lift at the mill warehouse.

Then he rented one of those little houses on Laurel and drove back to Stockton to tell his wife the good news. And Sheridan? Sheridan took Dave to her favorite lawyer who handed him divorce papers."

"Oops. He got himself a lawyer, I hope."

"Nope, no lawyer. Quit the job, abandoned the rental. Ran off to Alaska, where he worked on a fishing boat, as I recall. I think he had had enough fighting. I was so pissed at Sheridan. Mark was spooked about having a kid anyway. And now, here was his kid brother saddled with child support and no marriage."

"I see your problem."

Carolyne's tone was casual, almost sympathetic, but I sensed her instinctive cunning. She has a nose for things buried but not forgotten, for gossip and scandal. She's the only person I know who buys, carries home and actually reads those scandal sheets you find in supermarket checkout lines.

"My answer to what you call a problem is in there," I countered, perhaps unnecessarily, pointing toward Ty's bedroom.

"True," she conceded. "So, this Dave, is he bald too?"

I shook my head. "Not the last time I saw him."

"Who's bald?" Ty asked, entering the kitchen in the sweat pants he had slept in. He poured himself some coffee and sat down.

"Not you," Carolyne said, digging her fingers into his thick wavy hair.

"He got my dad's hair," I said. "Lucky boy."

Carolyne gave his head a shake. "Well, lucky boy, your uncle Dave is coming for the ceremony. It's a big deal."

"Uncle Dave? Cool."

Carolyne slid the plate of croissants toward him. "You remember him?"

Ty nodded; his mouth full of croissant. "Tahoe."

"After Alaska Dave operated a lift at Heavenly Valley for several years.," I explained to Carolyne.

"Baseball nut. Loves burgers," Ty said. "He knew where all the best burgers were and he would buy them as often as I wanted. Not fast burgers. Real burgers. So, is Cassidy coming?"

"No. Mark said he's in Iraq. Marines, I think." I turned to Carolyne, "So, when they came over from Stockton that Christmas...."

"What Christmas?" Ty asked.

"Our first Christmas at the Rose Cottage. I was telling Carolyne. Dave came to visit with Cassidy and his mother. Cassidy was just a toddler."

"So, I...."

"Wasn't," Carolyne said. "Not yet. A gleam in your daddy's eye maybe. Or, in this case, your mother's." She gave me a buttery grin.

"Do you remember the Rose Cottage?" I asked, ignoring her.

"Mom, I've told you a hundred times. I have no memory of the inside of that house. The outside I remember. You used to drive me past every chance you got. And Dad took me out to the homestead."

"The cabin? Mark took you out there?"

"Couple of times. He knows the people. They let us walk around."

"Really, I had no idea."

"He told me and Amanda that those years out there, that was the happiest time of his life."

"I can't believe he told you that."

Ty looked at Carolyne and shook his head. "It's tough. Dad still wants to be on the homestead. Mom still wants to be in the Rose Cottage. And now I learn they celebrated Christmas before I was born."

§

A few minutes later, when he was looking through one of the albums, Ty asked, "Mom, why did you and Dad sell the place? Well, both places, the homestead and the Rose Cottage. You loved both of them."

"Well, we sold the cabin to buy the Rose Cottage and...." I looked to Carolyne.

"They had to," she told him. "That's what happens. You divide up the assets. Your dad had his business, your mom had some retirement benefits built up at the district. They sort of equaled out. Then there was the equity in the house, the only thing of real value. Neither one could afford to buy the other out. So, you sell and divide the cash. And since you were dividing your time between them, child support was pretty much a wash."

Ty looked at her. "Ahh, you weren't involved, were you? Like Mom's attorney or something?"

Ty had pulled a coup. He had brought a momentary blush to Carolyne's face.

"Well, actually, I was your dad's attorney."

"Okay," Ty said slowly, putting his hand over his eyes. "Okay."

My magnificent son seemed to be collapsing over his coffee cup and I felt the need to restore him in some way.

"Ty, I...."

Carolyne shook her head and held up her hands to stop me. "Well, kid," she said brightly, "this *is* your graduation day."

"Right." He pushed back his chair and stood up. "You're both coming, aren't you?"

I was shocked. "Coming? Of course, we're coming. And we're picking up Grandma Ruth."

"Good," he said returning to his room, taking his cup and a second croissant with him.

"He didn't think we were coming?" I asked.

"He knew we were coming," Carolyne said.

§

The ceremony took place in the gymnasium at two in the afternoon. The sun was burning through the fog as we approached the building. Up ahead we saw Mark and Lynn with Amanda. They were following Dave and Grandma Eileen, Mark and Dave's mother, all of them moving slowly because Eileen needs a walker.

"Do we sit together?" I asked. "What's the protocol here?"

"We join them if there's room," Carolyne decided. "We are all Ty's family, after all. That's why we're here."

"Is that the best man?" my mother asked.

"Yes, that's Dave, I think."

"Looks well fed."

"Must be the burgers, Ruth," Carolyne said. "I hear there's been a lot of burgers."

We sat directly behind them. Ruth and Eileen remembered each other. They had both lost their husbands and had moved to the coast to be closer to their children.

"You still follow the game?" Dave asked me.

"Not really. Too much money and steroids. They all look like freaks to me now. One of the things I used to like was the bodies. Valenzuela looked like a store clerk, Willie McGee like a waif."

"You still got the ball?"

"With Willie's autograph? You bet."

"She keeps it in a case on the chest-of-drawers," Carolyne said. "I don't have the guts to even dust it."

"You should take it, Dave. You caught it."

"Naw, you got the signature. Besides, I got to grow up first, settle down."

"You could give it to Cassidy," I suggested just as the processional began.

Dave looked at me for a moment. "Will it to him," he said, and then turned around.

The graduates took their places on risers that had been set up on the stage. Ty was seated on the top row near one end. Amanda stood on her chair and waved to him but he didn't seem to notice her. Maybe it was the light.

"I wonder if he feels alone in the world," I whispered to Carolyne. Some of the kids were talking and jostling each other, but Ty sat quietly. He looked pensive. "We're an odd lot, when you think about it. All his life back and forth. The different houses. Then you and me, then Mark and Lynn. Then Amanda." I took my mother's hand and squeezed it. "My mom and dad were there for me, and I knew it. But we've just dragged him along with us. It must seem that way to him."

"He feels loved, Aurora. That should be obvious to you."

"I wish it were." My eyes were brimming suddenly. "He didn't know for sure we were coming!"

"Girls," Ruth admonished. "They're starting."

God, I thought, I'm sixteen again. My boyfriend is leaving for college and my mother is telling me to hush up and watch the TV.

§

Later at Mark and Lynn's I embarrassed Ty by bringing the photo albums in from the car. I thought, okay, you're one of those people with photo albums, be one of those people with photo albums.

"I never felt comfortable in that place," Mark said looking at a picture of the Rose Cottage. "After the cabin where we built everything, this was like a museum. I was afraid to pound a nail in a wall to hang a picture." To Lynn he said, "Did I ever tell you what the sellers gave us after the closing?" Then to me, "You remember?"

"Of course."

"A collage," he announced to everyone. "A framed collage made up of pieces of newsprint. The original builders had insulated the house with newspapers, stuffing them between the inner and outer walls. The sellers had discovered this during some repair work, and they had assembled some of the pieces into a collage. The papers dated from the Civil War!"

"That's kind of creepy," Lynn said, wrinkling her nose. "Lying in bed surrounded by old newspapers. Think of the fire danger."

"Exactly," Mark said. "Exactly."

I had treasured that collage. I had loved the idea of living in a house surrounded by newspapers a hundred and twenty years old. Seeing Mark and Lynn click like that made me realize that our marriage had been doomed from the beginning. We saw nothing eye to eye. One of the problems we constantly had was finding each other. We would separate while shopping and agree to meet at a certain place and time, and it would never work out. I always thought it was his fault and he always thought it was mine.

"Strapping lads," Dave said now. The photo showed him standing in deep snow with Cassidy on one side and Ty on the other. The three of them were aiming snowballs at the camera. "What? Seven and five, maybe?"

Mark looked at me. "Six and four?"

"Yeah, six and four." The year we separated, Mark had taken Ty to Tahoe to visit when Dave had Cassidy for a week at Christmas. We had sold the Rose Cottage by then. Our humble assets had been divided and I was living in a house on Perry devoid of character but close to the school Ty would attend.

"May I?" Eileen said. We handed her the photograph. She bent her head and peered at it over the top of her glasses. "I think of him every day, son."

"I know, Mom," Dave said. "So do I."

"Okay, guys," Ty said. "Enough of the baby crap. You're missing the good ones. Look at this."

It was a newspaper photo attached to an article. The headline read: Chandler Saves Two as Cats take Double Header.

"Whoa," Dave said.

"The stopper," I said. "Tying and winning runs on in the second game, nobody out. Ty comes in and strikes out the side."

"You get a scholarship with that?"

"No, Uncle Dave. I wasn't that good. Lucky day, I guess."

He flashed a grin, a young man pleased by his accomplishments, aware of his limitations, honest with himself. What more could a mushy mother want?

§

It was shortly before sunset when we dropped Ruth off at her apartment in the complex.

"Could you spare another hour?" I asked Carolyne.

"Of course. Is it what I think it is?"

"Maybe," I said. "And a little more."

We parked on a side street and walked to the edge of the driveway. The person Mark and I sold to had held on to the Rose Cottage for a couple of years. Then he sold it, and that person had sold it and so it had been. Somewhere along the line, somebody had built an ugly two-car garage in the front yard, ruining all the lines. It was a rental now, boats and trucks parked around, the lawn forgotten, the walls needing a fresh coat of paint.

The night Dave got back from Stockton with the divorce papers he came over for dinner. Mark was furious. Sheridan's lawyer had told Dave that she would get the house and custody and more child support than he could afford. If he fought it would just cost him more. "But she left you!" Mark kept saying.

I took Carolyne's hand. "Walk with me," I said.

We took a trail to the headlands where a cool breeze was coming in off the water. We made our way down a narrow path to the beach and crossed the small stream, jumping the pattern of exposed stones. A driftwood fire blazed at the other end of the beach where a dozen young people were clustered. Graduates maybe.

"I'm sorry. We should have at least changed our shoes," I said.

"It's all right. It's getting firmer as we go out."

Dave had left after dinner and Mark had gone to a meeting on the salmon rearing project, one of the many community efforts he has been involved with over the years. I had always known he would be a good father. He was stable, dependable, loving in his way. But I saw my future disappearing that night. After what had happened to Dave, I thought Mark would never choose to have a child. It was February and well after dark. After I cleaned up the dishes I had taken the flashlight and followed the path Carolyne and I were taking now.

She and I stopped where I had stopped. We stood at the edge of the water in the shadow of a large guano-covered outcropping that stands off shore just beyond low tide. It must have been part of the headland at some point but the ancient flowing stream and the beating of the tides had left it standing there alone.

"Have you ever used a diaphragm?" I asked Carolyne.

"A diaphragm? Tell me, why would I use a diaphragm?"

"Right. Well, I did. For years. About three years into the pill I began to bleed, a lot. The doctor had me switch to the diaphragm."

"Okay, so why are you asking me this?"

Good question. The clouds were yellow above the setting sun and their reflection in the gentle surf was so luminous, so true, that it appeared as a thin gold plating that reproduced perfectly each ripple in each expended wave. I felt released and dangerously giddy.

"I don't know. I thought about the smell for some reason. To make sure the barrier works, you coat it with this gel-like spermicide. The stuff smells. You put a little on your hands and you can smell it, even if you wash."

Carolyne started to laugh. "You brought me down here to tell me that spermicide stinks?"

"I brought you down here to show you this spot, okay? This spot was important to me. This is where I would come when Mark and I were having problems. I made decisions here. Big decisions."

"Sorry!"

"I'm processing, okay? My son has graduated from high school. It's the end of an era. I got out the stupid albums and now I'm standing here where I used to stand when he was young. The night he was conceived I stood here."

"Okay!"

"That's all. That's all there is to it."

"Okay," Carolyne said. "Okay."

The sun dropped below the horizon and drew the color from the sky, leaving the water a cold gray. The wind stiffened and turned slightly so it was blowing more out of the north. I could smell the smoke from the fire up the beach where the young people were celebrating.

THE YELLOW SCARF

Three days after I took Joan to meet my parents, I abandoned her at a party. That juxtaposition is not my creation. I mean, I didn't think, at the time, that what happened at the party really amounted to my abandoning her; nor did I notice any particular significance in the fact that the abandonment, if that's what it was, happened so soon after the weekend with my parents. Joan pointed all that out later. She found meaning there, you might say. I reminded her that we did have an understanding, that I had made myself clear about commitments from the beginning. She shrugged and said something about how the truth could be obliterated with explanations.

The occasion that allowed me to introduce Joan to my parents was the marriage of Brenda my kid sister to a guy named Carl she'd met in college. The ceremony took place at the house up in Humboldt County where my parents moved after they retired. The country up there is beautiful—forested hills everywhere you look, the sky clean and open, no traffic. Joan and I took a vacation day on Friday and meandered through wine country on the way up. She had arranged for her son Sean to stay with his father so we could be alone.

The wedding took place at two on Saturday afternoon, and I have to say I was moved to see Brenda in the same white gown our mother and her two older sisters had worn at their weddings. An end, you could say, as much as a beginning. When I married Rhonda ten years earlier, Brenda had been the flower girl. Rhonda and I got married at the house in Emeryville where her parents lived at the time. That house had a beautiful curving staircase that descended into the living room. The wedding took place at night, the lights off, a row of candles lighted along the banister, very nice. The idea was for the bridal party to make its grand entrance down the stairs, and Brenda, who was eight at the time, would lead the way, sprinkling rose petals as she went. But Brenda got it into her head to make sure that at least one petal fell on every step. I don't know if you've ever tried to throw a rose petal, but for accuracy they're zero. Kenny Stabler couldn't throw a rose petal to his intended receiver if the guy was standing two feet away. So, the procession was interminable. A friend of ours was playing a Bach polonaise on the flute and she had to play through it a dozen times before we could get Brenda off the stairs.

No stairway for Brenda and her Carl. They were married outside in the garden where our mother, a plant freak, had everything blooming. As I watched Brenda and Dad pass beneath the arbor weighted down with jasmine and make their way to the patch of variegated tulips, I felt sad that my daughter Tasha, who is nine, could not be there. It would have been a fitting closure, it seemed to me, had she been Brenda's flower girl. But Tasha is in Chicago with her mother. Rhonda took her back there even before the divorce became final.

Joan fit in very well with the family, a fact that she thought had some bearing on what happened later. Ours is an open, generous family in many ways, but I was a little worried because Rhonda had been a real favorite. And everyone, I guess, was eager to see just who I was involved with now that the marriage had ended. Of course, that is not what I had intended, really, when I brought Joan to the wedding. It wasn't like an announcement of a commitment or something, though in retrospect, I realize it wasn't just a night out at the movies either.

§

The office where I work in Oakland is located over an auto parts store. Basically, it is one large room that formerly served as a dance studio. We installed partitions and lighting, and now it has a reception room, a corner for the secretaries and five individual offices. The offices are cramped and carpeted with remnants; the walls are pervious to sounds as slight as a dropped pen and covered with posters and quotes from Gibran, Cleaver and "Desiderata." It gets too hot in the winter and smells of coffee and mimeograph fluid and, before we outlawed them, cigarette smoke. Typewriters clatter, people laugh and curse and everywhere is clutter. The office tends to reflect that social change—which is what we do—is seldom precise, only abstractly measurable and never tidy.

But from this confusion of noise and smells and action must arise precise understandable accountings of what funds come in and what go out. Grants, both public and private, provide our sustenance, and new grants become available only if the old ones are carefully and precisely accounted for. To the penny. Take last summer's swim program. I can show you where every dollar went. I can tell you exactly how many kids took the program, the number who learned to swim and how well. I can provide a to-the-dollar figure on what it cost us to teach one child to swim. That said, Denise and Tyrone who ran that program couldn't care less about the numbers. To them, the experience involved values unconnected to dollars and even to swimming, but as administrator, I have to know the numbers.

I'm explaining this because it leads to Joan. We hired Joan—I hired Joan—to transform the messy and the vibrant into the orderly and the tidy, the conversion of life into numbers. And I hired her because of her clothes. I knew what I was looking for and when she came in for an interview, I knew she was the one. Her outfit wasn't elegant or particularly expensive. She wore slacks and as I recall a blouse that had some quiet embroidery on the yoke. But it was all neat, trim, cautious browns and tans thoughtfully blended. Sensible shoes, her dark hair neither long nor short but vibrant and nicely shaped. The zinger was a silk scarf of bright yellow draped around her neck. That scarf, both casual and luxurious, seemed somehow daring, given the balance of her attire. It represented a bridge between the fastidious and the flamboyant, the carefully aligned column of numbers and the confusion in the street. I knew she would be both dependable and decisive. To illustrate my respect, I gave her the one office with a decent view.

That was two years ago. Joan assumed her duties with enthusiasm, and, as I hoped, she had a passion for accuracy, a trait not common in my line of work. I did not know it at the time, but she had only recently separated from her husband, and she needed the job both for the money and for the therapy that our vibrant workplace provided. (Her husband had left the country to seek enlightenment, and her son, Sean, who was two at the time, was often sick with ear infections.)

In that respect she was a year ahead of me. When Joan came on board, my marriage to Rhonda was only beginning to unravel; the process was slow, complicated and at times as painful as slapping a boil. No purpose would be served by going into that history except to say I frequently found myself sitting in Joan's office trying to make sense of what was going on. I gravitated there because, as I had seen from the beginning, Joan had the ability to find order in the disorderly.

Her office became a refuge. How she made it quiet in there, or why it smelled so fresh, remains a mystery to me. Nor do I understand where she stashed all the reports, charts, memoranda, directives and grant applications that entered the door. Her desk looked like a rink of newly formed ice with its brown telephone in one corner, a calculator, a mechanical pencil, a legal pad, a few papers neatly stacked; resting on a folded paper towel, a hand-thrown ceramic cup gave off the aroma of chamomile. She had painted the walls soft yellows and quiet browns. No posters, no quotes; just two photos of her son, one abstract woven tapestry. Probably a dozen plants were set about: cactus and coleus on the windowsill, a spider plant and a Swedish ivy hanging from hooks and cascading toward the floor.

§

We became friends. But then the office is a friendly place. I encourage that. After work on Fridays most of us play shuffleboard in a bar down the street. We have a party the week before Christmas and do a gift draw. Labor Day we picnic at Lake Merritt. The day my divorce became final the gang got me ripping drunk on Cold Duck. Two things I'll never do again: get drunk on Cold Duck or get divorced.

One night Joan had several of us over for dinner. She lives in a small house off 35th Street in Oakland. It's a pleasant lower-middle-class neighborhood, some Blacks, some Whites, a few Hispanics. Around the corner from her place a Japanese family has transformed their small front yard into one of those gardens where white gravel is raked to look like water swirling around random islands of black stone. Small jade plants set in the corners.

I learned this because while Joan was preparing the meal, I took her dog for its evening constitutional. The dog is named Emily. I was surprised to learn Joan had a dog. Dogs can be sloppy, especially a silver-gray dustmop on four legs like Emily, and I could not image Joan tolerating the clutter or mess that having a dog entails. A tiny thing, Emily's hair parts along her back, her eyes are onyx marbles protruding above a shiny black nose. When she meets a person or another dog, she either growls or rolls over and sticks her feet in the air. When she met me, she did both. Sean joined me on the walk because he knows the country, so to speak.

A week or so later, Joan asked me over for dinner, this time just her, me, Sean and Emily. She baked lasagna and I brought a bottle of chianti. After Sean was asleep we took Emily for a walk. The night was cool with a low damp fog; the kind of night where sounds are magnified and the stillness seems to possess a texture that you can feel. We walked a long way in and around the neighborhood, and she told me about her marriage and about another fellow she lived with for six months after the marriage ended. Her husband had joined a religious movement; he went to India for a year where he and hundreds of other devotees groveled outside the guru's house awaiting a blessing from the master's lips. He's back now, selling used cars in Marin and doing very well. The other fellow is an actor, a dynamic, intense guy, or so I understood, who unfortunately for Joan, fell in love with a male rock singer and moved out.

I was amazed to hear all this "past" flowing from the lips of my fiscal officer. Not that her experiences were atypical of the times. What amazed me was my own ignorance. For months I had been pouring out my troubles to her without bothering to learn the most basic facts of her existence. That evening we achieved a sort of parity, it seemed to me, and Joan acquired a dimension, I had not recognized before.

§

Since separating from Rhonda, I have lived alone on Clay Street in San Francisco. I rent a small, third-floor apartment with a kitchen, two rooms and a bath. It has creaking hardwood floors, countless layers of paint on the walls, and a bell that rings when someone pushes a button on the mailbox. The neighborhood kids love to push the buttons late at night, and sometimes the bell in my apartment sticks on. It happened the first time around midnight on a Saturday night. The sound was horrible. It rang for sixteen hours before the landlord, a small Chinese man who never smiles, came over and fixed it. He showed me how to turn it off. The other tenants are elderly, most are Chinese. I know none of them. I hear their doors opening and closing, their feet padding along the corridor. Occasionally, I meet them on the stairs. They peer at me with watery intelligent eyes. We nod.

I don't really know why I remain in this apartment except I hate the thought of moving. This may sound ironic considering my line of work, but personally I am tiring of change. Also, the view is very nice. Off the kitchen at the back is a fire escape landing. There's no door but I can easily step out through the window. On the grated landing I have placed a chair on a square of plywood. Some evenings I tune into a classical music station, tote a glass of cream sherry out the window and watch the sun set over San Francisco. Thousands of pastel houses line the hills to the south and west; I smell soy sauce and hot cooking oil.

I started going to Joan's house once in a while after work. With my daughter Tasha back in Chicago, I transformed some of the loss I felt for her into affection for Sean. In the backyard I pushed him on the swing and threw sticks for Emily. Neither ever seemed to get tired of this. Throw a stick in a bush and Emily will half kill herself getting it out. Some evenings I stayed with Sean when Joan went out for the evening.

One night I stayed over, it just happened.

§

I travel now and then in connection with my work, conferences, workshops. I drive to Sacramento regularly, fly to Denver, Chicago. Two or three times a year I'm in Washington and New York. It's vital, I believe. A track record, careful accounting, creative ideas, well-crafted applications are all important, but you have to be known by the people you're dealing with. They're more comfortable giving money to a familiar face, a remembered joke. I flew east the morning after I spent that first night with Joan. It was an unfortunate coincidence but the trip had been scheduled for some time. On my way back I stopped off in Chicago and spent the day with Tasha.

But Joan was on my mind, and the day I returned I took her out for a drink. As usual, I did most of the talking. She knew much of it, of course, but I went deeper. It's surprising how much there is when you really go into it. She knew Rhonda and I were high-school sweethearts and that we had married when I was nineteen. What she did not know was that Rhonda was pregnant at the time, or that, except for Rhonda, I had never enjoyed a serious relationship with a woman. I told Joan that the kid who married Rhonda is now a stranger to me.

We were in a tavern not far from her house, a working-class joint with country music on the jukebox and pickled eggs in a jar on the bar. Joan and the actor used to go there. I wanted a clear understanding before we went any further, and I had a double bourbon to prepare myself. I told her I cared very much for her. Then I had a second bourbon and I told her that in one lifetime, one divorce is enough. Some jerk kept playing the same song on the jukebox, a drone filled with sentimental slop. Each time it came on, she winced. I thought maybe it reminded her of the actor and I regretted bringing her to that place. Later I understood more was involved.

Joan was quiet, more quiet than usual, though she said she understood about the divorce. She said she too was cautious about serious emotional commitments. I relaxed for the first time in four days. We finished our drinks, picked up Sean and went out to dinner. Hamburgers and fries. Sean picked the restaurant.

§

That was six months before Brenda's wedding, and in the weeks that followed I tried to be sensitive to Joan's situation. I sensed a fragility there. I wanted to respect her integrity, her personal space. But I work long hours and it was easy, perhaps too easy, to drop by her house. Whenever I went, I brought food or wine. I always did the dishes, and when I stayed over I helped make the bed. Joan is the only person I've met other than my mother who makes the bed every day. That may be why they got along so well: bedmakers and plant freaks. Later she made an issue of how casually I stopped by the house. As she pointed out, it's true that she never came unannounced to my apartment but the comparison is not really fair. Her place is much closer to the office and because of Sean and Emily she is more attached to her home than I am to mine. Besides, she often *invited* me over. She *wanted* me there, after all. But these are specious arguments. In truth, it was cozy there, a house where a family lived. And I very much enjoyed her company.

Joan has a number of friends, several of whom I met, but I knew she was not involved with anyone else. We never talked about that aspect of our lives, but I knew. In her bedroom she had set up a small loom, and she attended weaving classes two nights a week. Her yarn was carefully stored in a wicker basket. Nothing was left lying around. Sometimes, when the babysitting arrangement fell through, she asked if I would stay with Sean while she went to class. I always did what I could. He's a kind, delicate child. Once, when Joan gave him some money to buy a toy, he bought me a present instead, a magnetized plastic gadget that holds coins. I attached it to my dashboard and have coins available for parking meters.

Except for work, my life during this period was fairly quiet. I did have one other female acquaintance, a woman I met as Rhonda and I were breaking up. At that time she worked for the Marin Housing Authority. Eventually, she quit and moved to a small house near

Marshall on the coast. At first it was pretty intense between us but now we're just friends. She spends most of her time taking self-improvement courses and altering her diet in various ways. Her wealthy parents live in Connecticut; her father is involved on Wall Street: law firm, investment house. I've never learned the details, but they send her enough to be comfortable. She owns a small sailboat and we went out into Tamales Bay a couple of times. The last time I saw her was a couple of months before Brenda's wedding. The day was calm, clear, and we were lolling with a limp sail in the middle of the bay when she said she was thinking about having a baby. I thought of Joan struggling to raise her son. I had the impression that motherhood was the one thing my bored friend had yet to try.

§

There is no question but that Joan and I had a great time together during the weekend of the wedding. We left my parents' house early Sunday morning and drove south along the coast. We had lunch in Mendocino and later made love in the golden grass above a lonely stretch of Route One. We could see the shoreline for miles.

§

Some of the Bay Area legal aid people sponsored a workshop for the Monday after Brenda's wedding. I had arranged for Joan and me to attend as representatives from our office. This reflected Joan's position in the office, not her relationship with me. During the previous two years her importance had grown steadily. Her recommendations were carefully considered. Her insistence on clarity, her grasp of financial risks and opportunities, her comfort with detail had proven invaluable. She had become my right arm.

The workshop held at the Saint Francis Hotel was entitled "Social Change—New Directions for the Eighties." I was scheduled to moderate a session on funding, but the star of the show was the keynote speaker Eileen Rueben. I've changed the name, of course, but anyone who has played my game for any length of time knows about Ms. Reuben. At the age of twenty-one she was a Peace Corps Volunteer in a small village high in the Bolivian Andes. The village people were poor and indigenous. They survived by raising a few sheep and alpacas and tilling their rocky soil. The women wove but the quality of their product was low. Eileen Reuben revolutionized that community. She introduced new weaving methods; she created powerful designs from traditional motifs and incorporated them in a line of sweaters, scarves and hats. She established a marketing cooperative and found distributors as far away as Europe and the United States. The techniques Reuben developed in Bolivia are now taught in community development courses all across this county. Later, she was active in the anti-war movement, and then with migrant workers in the Carolinas. I once saw a photo of her standing in a potato field, an enraged farmer jamming a shotgun against her neck. Now she works for ACTION. In my business, Eileen Reuben is a legend.

I had, as I mentioned, seen a photograph or two, but before the workshop I had never met her. And of what efficacy are photographs for restraining the imagination? I envisioned a Jewish dynamo from the Big Apple with a voice like a criminal defense lawyer and arms like a Russian streetsweeper. In the elevator I gave Joan my prediction: Eileen Reuben would slap her briefcase down on the table and introduce herself in short clipped sentences that would sound like a saw grinding it way through the barrel of a Sherman tank. Joan just smiled. I've been to enough of these workshops to no longer take them seriously. But when it comes to work, if Joan is anything, serious describes it. She had already offered to prepare a synopsis for the rest of the staff.

§

Eileen Reuben knew all about the rent strike I organized in Alameda! That was the first thing she mentioned when we were introduced. And she said that people in Washington still talk about the methods I devised to fight redlining.

I stuttered; I smiled without cause; I called Bolivia Brazil. She was tall and thin with eyes like gray fog and a voice that purred. No doubting the power there, the sense of independence and exquisite control, but it came across so gently.

That evening was the party, the one I alluded to at the beginning. I would not say I "abandoned" Joan. That was her terminology. In a certain sense you could say we were not really at the party together at all. It's true I drove us to the workshop and then to the party, but it's office practice to pool cars whenever possible—and she knew several people at the party in addition to me. Even as I write this I realize how picky I sound.

Eileen and I had a number of mutual friends scattered around the country. As she said, it really was remarkable that we had not met before. Something I did not know: she was also divorced. She, too, had married young and was divorced even before she went to Bolivia. She said the best thing about her present situation was that it left open the possibility of what she called "adventurous intimacy." Another amazing thing: Eileen Reuben was crazy about Chinese food, especially Szechuan. I knew several really great places. She understood, before we left the party that I would drive my colleague home. But when I went to find Joan she was gone. I later learned that she had taken a bus back to Oakland.

Eileen was scheduled on a midnight flight to Washington. At eleven she called and rescheduled for nine in the morning. We were sitting in a pub at the time, sipping cognac. At eight in the morning she called again and rescheduled for six that evening. Then we both called our offices. Though in fact I felt wonderful, I claimed I was too sick to come in, something I had never done before in my life. Later, we took the ferry across to Sausalito, had lunch and went shopping. Sometime during the day, I can't describe exactly how or when, Eileen Reuben began to leave. The lightness, the laughter, the close attention seemed to fade away, leaving in their absence a distracted formality, a human being on automatic pilot. On the way to the airport we hit heavy traffic. In the stop and go Eileen pulled a vial from her purse. She looked tired, her mouth tight, her mood distant. The legend popped two pills into her mouth and needed no water to get them down. We arrived at SFO with just moments to spare. When I got back to my car I found a ticket on my windshield, and the clouds that had been rolling in all afternoon were letting down a soft drizzle. I ended up drinking too much in a bar on Columbus Avenue. By seven the next morning I was at work. I had missed Friday, then Monday and Tuesday and my desk was covered with mail to answer and phone messages to return. At midmorning I polished my courage and walked into Joan's office. She wasn't there. Lois, our receptionist and timekeeper, said Joan had called in yesterday and requested a couple of days off. I called her home. No answer. I went back to the clutter on my desk where I found a message from Al Raby. Al wanted me to call. He and I had worked together on the rent strike years ago. Now he is the director of CETA in a neighboring county.

I need to tell you this about Al Raby. Al Raby has one of those booming deep black booming voices that, well, it is inconceivable that anyone has ever said "Huh?" to Al Raby. He came on the phone and thundered into my ear: "We've got a really good position open over here, assistant to the director. One of your people, Joan Meyer, has applied for it. I interviewed her yesterday. I think she's got the job but I wanted to call…"

"Joan Meyer! No, Al, no. Joan is the heart of my operation, Al!"

Raby's laugh may be the most cynical sound in the universe. During the rent strike I used to run into his office when I heard him on the phone with a landlord just so I could hear that laugh. You could almost feel the chill running down the poor landowner's spine.

Al Raby was laughing like that now. "That good is she?" The laughter rolling like thunder. "I suspected as much but I wanted to check with you."

"You thief! You body snatcher!"

§

I tried again to call Joan, but there was still no answer. The office was a madhouse. A line of people waited to see me. The telephone kept ringing. It was ten at night before I could get away. I found her standing on a corner near her house, hands in the pockets of her coat, a leash emerging from one. Emily at the other end sniffing a clump of grass.

We must have walked for miles. This time it was her turn to talk, and she had plenty to say, some of which I have indicated. We traversed as many emotions as streets. Beneath a streetlight I noticed her cheeks were shining, but the prevailing emotion I got from her was determination. She told me how much she cared for me. It was the first time either of us had spoken of love. Then she revealed something I thought I would never hear from steady, dependable Joan. During the first six weeks after her husband ran off to India leaving her with Sean, she had considered suicide. She said she had simply no vision of herself independent of a man. But now it was different. Now she had a vision. She had built it slowly and painfully, piece by piece. No man, she told me, not even one she loved, would ever take that vision away from her.

I will admit that I begged her to return to the office. I promised everything I could offer and more. But she refused. The position with Al Raby was an excellent opportunity for her and she knew it. She did agree to go on seeing me, but since there were no commitments, it would be on a dating basis. I should always call before I came over. We said goodnight at her front door.

When I arrived at Clay Street the front bell was ringing. I heard it at the bottom of the stairs and it grew louder with every step I climbed. I found a screwdriver and managed to turn it off. In the sink beneath a pool of gray water were the dishes from Eileen's and my breakfast. Outside the back window a thousand lights sparkled in the city. As I washed the dishes, I found myself whistling. We had lost an irreplaceable fiscal officer, but I did have a date for Friday evening.

LAB REPORT

When we peeled back our blinders, our shapers and definers, we discovered Pure Love. Yes, truly, there it was, a glob of it on the exam table. To our delight it lingered, permitting delicate probes, sensors linked to instruments, hushed calculations, whispered conjectures, all confirming its vitality.

As *unique* admits no degree, so this substance permitted no metaphor and emitted none. More strange, that which is said to create all form using molecules, atoms, electrons and quarks was itself found to possess none.

Discovery-giddy now, and cocksure of control, when we squeezed the substance to fit a definition, it abruptly disappeared leaving no smear, no stain.

Gone.

WOMEN IN CAVES

She's in a warm room with soft light, the air smelling of chai. Someone must have brought her tea. Strong hands massage the soles of her feet. Her fingers are being manicured. A voice extols the virtues of a mud bath. "It will open your pores," the voice purrs. "You will be indulged as never before." Imagine! Floating up to your neck in warm mud.

"It's a great morning, Mom!"

Her husband has entered the bedroom, waking her from a state of bliss. Of course he would say it's a great morning, she thinks, smelling the coffee he sets on her nightstand. What else could he say? This is the first Saturday in April. This is the morning of the long awaited—by her husband that is—"Maiden Voyage."

§

During the winter just passed, the winter of 1979, Sheri Gardner's husband built a camper. He installed a woodstove in the garage and worked out there nights, weekends, and when stormy weather kept him off the backhoe, those days as well. The project absorbed much of the fall and winter.

Drawings and catalogs spread across the dining room table, sawdust sticking to the shower walls and drifting like wisps of sand across the kitchen floor. Her husband out in the garage most every night. Well, not on Wednesdays. The Boy Scouts meet on Wednesdays and Willie is scoutmaster and a former Eagle Scout himself. And twice a month on Tuesdays the firemen get together to train the crew and test the equipment. Willie's no longer chief, hasn't been for over a year, but the stationhouse, they say, would close without him. He knows where everything is and how everything works. He's familiar with the hydrant locations and the amount of pressure available at each and where to set up to attack a fire in a particular house. Nine times out of ten he can tell you the floor plan. He'd dug the foundation or trenched the leach lines or picked their daughter up at that house after a birthday party back when she was six.

A Friday night about ten Sheri goes out to the garage. She's fresh from a shower, a red robe over her nightgown, boots pulled on at the door so she can slosh through the wet grass, a spray of perfume behind the ears. Willie tells her to put her hand on the stovepipe. That's not where she was thinking to put it. Besides, the fire is roaring. She hesitates, her pale well-ringed hand extended, nails painted, jangles on the wrist. "Go on, put your hand on it." He's grinning, confident. And he's right, the pipe's not burning hot, just comfortably warm. "That's double-wall insulated pipe," he tells her. "Now give it a good shove. Go on, shove it." She shoves hard, thinking she'll show him, but nothing moves. "Built to code," he explains. "Braced inside and out with proper distances from the wall and a proper height above the roof to insure a good draft." Then he tells her to go back in the house, that he needs to finish just one little thing.

Sheri's asleep on the couch by the time he comes in, robe still wrapped around her, the TV spewing bad news from one part of the globe or another.

§

This morning the temperature is in the forties. River fog has the redwoods dripping a cold gray substance that when it touches the skin feels like ice. An earring has caught on something and she can't fix it because both arms are straining to hold a box of food and cooking utensils. She's snuggled deep inside the heaviest hooded sweatshirt she could find. Beneath her slacks and blouse is a set of thermal underwear that Willie bought her for Christmas five years ago. Thermal underwear! The least romantic form of lingerie a man could ever give a woman. And she's shivering. She's shivering enough to make the pans rattle.

Willie comes running out of the garage wearing a T-shirt and jeans. He hops in the truck holding the new camper and backs it up to the beach-buggy trailer. The bright blue tarp covering the buggy has been folded and put away. The whip antenna has been reinstalled to its place of honor, a new orange flag attached to the tip.

Sheri mutters the introductions: "Beloved Camper, I want you to meet Beloved Buggy." And she wishes, she really wishes, she was still in bed. Wherever that dream is, that's where she wants to be.

Willie jumps from the truck. "Mom, are the kids ready?" Then he's off to the garage without a glance in her direction, returning with two gasoline cans.

"Christ. We should've stashed this stuff days ago. The boys are waiting and I don't want to be late. Are they ready?"

"They said they were. This box...."

"Belinda! Brad!" Willie yells. "Let's go!"

It's Bel who presents herself first on the deck. Their daughter has a cassette player in her hand so as to surround herself with an atmosphere of jarring noise. She's wearing a pink halter and white shorts.

"Jesus Christ, she can't wear that." Willie's whisper suggests a state secret. "She's only fourteen for Christ's sake." He glances furtively at Bel from the corners of his eyes. "Mom, tell her to put something on."

84

Sheri hears the plea in her husband's voice but doesn't bite. As Bel flounces down the steps she is both appalled and thrilled at the sight.

"Time to get dressed, daughter. We're leaving." Willie makes himself busy hoisting the gasoline cans onto the buggy trailer.

"I am dressed." Bel moves closer to her father. The noise from the cassette player is unbearable.

"This is April, Bel. We're going on a camping trip." He's staying focused on the bungee cord, getting it tight around the cans.

"I got as much on as you and Mr. Landry at school says girls don't need much clothes cause girls got subcutaneous fat."

Willie's still not looking but he is turning a dangerous red. "Get your butt back inside, Bel. I want to see slacks on the bottom and a sweatshirt on the top. And do it quick. We're late. And while you're in there send your brother out."

Bel's expression reveals a surly sense of elation and her return walk to the house is reminiscent of a runway scene in the Miss America Pageant.

"Jesus Christ. As if it's subcutaneous fat she's showing to the world."

"What am I supposed to do with these?"

"Those are cooking things. They go in the camper."

"Am I actually permitted inside the glorious camper?"

Willie takes the box. "Okay, get in the truck. I'll deal with it."

"Does that mean I'm not permitted in the camper?"

"That means if I want something done I'd better do it myself."

It's Brad who appears now on the deck. Their son makes a pale and sullen statement buried in a gray sweatshirt and camouflage slacks, slumped beneath a bush hat. He carries a walkie-talkie. Now and then he holds it to his ear but no one is calling. No one ever calls.

"All right, son," Willie says with carefully manufactured cheer. "Bout ready to roll."

"Where's my mini-bike? Why isn't it tied on here?" Brad points at the front bumper of the truck.

"Want to take your bike? Good idea. Go get it."

"Can't you get it? You're closer."

"If you want it, Brad, get it out here."

Brad shoves the walkie-talkie at his mother. "And don't drop it." Moments later he's shouting from the garage. "Tires are flat. Both of 'em. And it's filthy."

"Christ." Willie descends the nifty little stairs he built off the back of the camper and heads toward the garage.

"Mom, will you come in here and clean off my bike?"

But Sheri has escaped into the cab of the truck. It's a little warmer in there and with the door closed and the window up she can pretend she doesn't hear.

§

Willie Gardner is behind the wheel and the family is flying along the winding road pulling the beach buggy on its well-packed trailer. Sheri is belted in the passenger seat and the reluctant kids are stowed in the camper. "Rounded up and locked away," as Willie put it.

"Look at that patch of blue, Mom. It's going to clear off!" Her husband is experiencing a rush of endorphins and he gives the steering wheel an enthusiastic slap. "She handles well, I tell you. Doesn't feel top-heavy or sluggish. Pickup is reasonable, given the weight. Sure glad I installed those heavy-duty shocks. We'd be swaying like a drunk without them. And the buggy is tracking nicely on the curves. Yep, it's a go."

Sheri slumps back in the seat, her eyes squint down to slits. She's trying to revive her warm and cozy bed. Manage an astral journey into the sheets. Leave the body in the truck as a decoy for Willie to talk to. She slides her astral hands beneath the pillow, her astral ear snuggles down into the feathery warmth, her astral knees curl up close to her astral chin, she can almost smell the chai....

"This is the Spider calling the Captain. You read me?" The CB has the snarl of a chronically enraged beast.

Willie grabs the microphone. "Spider guy! Ready to roll? Over."

"Mike's here. We've been set to roll for half an hour. Where are you? Over."

"Three minutes away and flying high. Better have your engines warm. Over and out."

It's the Boys, thinks Sheri Gardner, the much-loved Boys. There's Captain Willie's surly sidekick Spider Webb, the husband of Good Wife Dot. An infant born to the name Alvin, but never call him that, grown to a gnarly adulthood; too short to be happy but never tell him that, muscles taut as bridge cables that can never relax and a personality best described as pissed. A man who shares a name with a creature most humans find abhorrent. And with him, as always, the less-than-trusty aide-de-camp Needy Mike the Recently Jilted.

"I'm freezing."

Willie loves a fresh breeze when roaring down a road. To somewhat appease his wife he rolls his window up part way and flicks on the heater.

"Crack that rear window, Mom, and check on the kids. I built it so we could see what's going on back there."

"If I look away from the road I'll barf all over the seat."

"No matter. They're probably up in the bed anyway, looking out the little window. Great view from up there. See how she floats through these curves? Drives like a sports car once you get the hang of it."

They approach the home of Spider and Dot Webb and see the two rigs waiting in the driveway. Being a good wife, Dot is already sitting in the pickup. Spider and Mike, leaning on a fender, expect Willie to stop but he roars past, hand on the horn. Seeing the troops rush for their trucks gives him a good chuckle.

There is no hope for it Sheri sees now. The forces are assembled and the sun is burning through the fog. The convoy advances on the ocean, whipping through the curves, antennas swept back, orange flags flapping, all the toys in a line. For Willie Gardner it gets no better than this. He lets out a yell that sets Sheri's ears to ringing. You'd think he was shoulder to shoulder with George Pickett and they were thundering up the hill at Gettysburg.

§

Sheri clutches the handle above the window as Willie leaves the pavement and steers the convoy past a cluster of campers at the edge of the beach. He follows a sandy uneven road northward half a mile to their campsite, a relatively isolated spot near the mouth of Windy Creek.

When the bouncing finally stops and Sheri has released her grip she hears pounding on the window behind her. Pressed against the glass is the face of her frantic daughter.

"Get me out of here!" Bel shouts. "Get me out of here!"

Willie Gardner is not concerned with the passengers in the rear. He's out of the cab and across the sand to reconnoiter with the Spider and Needy Mike. Mike has pulled his rig up against the bluff. He's walking around with a quart of beer in his hand. Bel continues to pound on the glass.

"Get me out of here!"

Willie really does have the door at the back of the camper locked from the outside! Sheri can't believe it. Behind the door her daughter is pounding away. "Get me out of here!"

Sheri tells her daughter to have a little patience, that she needs to get the key. She turns to see Needy Mike heave his bottle against some rocks at the base of the bluff. A shower of suds and brown glass blossoms in front of him.

Okay, Sheri thinks, now that's nice. That's real nice.

The hefty form of Good Wife Dot is running toward her through the sand, erratic in her movements, puffing with exertion. Belinda is pounding on the door. Needy Mike is staring at the rocks and his lost beer. Willie is staring at Needy Mike and Spider Webb is kicking the sand with one of his lower appendages as if he were trying to stamp out a brush fire.

"Linda's here!" the Good Wife gasps. "Back at the road. Camped with Rod Blessing."

"Let me out of here!"

"Linda, here?"

The head of Good Wife Dot bobs rapidly up and down.

Sheri experiences a flood of surprising rage. "Here? I mean, why here? If she dumped Mike and all. Why isn't she home in bed, or out shopping, or at a spa somewhere? What's she doing back here?"

"Mom! Help me!"

Well..." Dot seems stunned by the thoughts Sheri is expressing.

Belinda is pounding with both fists.

"And Rod Blessing?" Sheri has to yell above the surf and her daughter's screams, "Rod Blessing? Rod Blessing is Mike with less money and no more brains."

"Well...Spider says this is our turf. Linda knows that."

"I can't believe it. Rod Blessing."

"Mommm!"

"Bel, relax. I have to get the key."

§

Incoming tide and the surf's pounding. Willie can't hear her though he stands only a few feet away. Her voice powerless, Sheri feels powerless herself. Everything around her has taken on an immense size, clarity and strength. The sand goes on forever, the huge dark bluff, the enormous sea beating on beach and rock, the spreading cloud of mist. The air itself is an enormous sponge absorbing her voice.

"Mommm!"

Her feet have sunk into the sand and she can hardly walk. The earring is caught again in the hood of her sweatshirt ripping at the lobe. She has to look the complete fool, she thinks, a hapless monk who has wandered away from his cloister and can't find the way back.

"Willie! Where's the key!" She touches his shoulder.

"Linda's here."

"I know. I need the key. Bel's frantic."

"Mike's upset." Willie jerks his head stealthily toward Needy Mike as if they were standing outside a cage at the zoo and he doesn't want to disturb the primates. The subject of their attention is pacing back and forth past the dripping rocks, mourning his lost love, his lost beer. "Spider too."

"The key, Willie. I need the key."

"She's a bitch," Spider announces.

"You've got the key. Remember? I gave you a key. I put it on your key ring. It's the little silver one next to the key to the pickup."

Sheri does not remember any of this but it does sound like something Willie would do. He would have come in some night when she was half asleep on the couch and he would have explained how he had installed a lock on the back of the camper and how he'd had an extra key made and he was giving it to her and here give me your purse and I'll put it on the ring and there now you have it right next to the pickup key so if you ever need to get into the camper you can. And this in the midst of one of her favorite programs.

Spider Webb continues his assessment: "Blessing's a punk."

"I didn't bring my keys."

"I see. You didn't bring your keys."

"Maybe we should go back there, eh Willie?" Spider takes another swipe at the sand with his boot.

Willie smiles a benign smile. "Just so you know, there's another set of keys hidden on the truck. One for the camper rear door and another that opens the truck doors and operates the ignition. They're in a little magnetic box that's stuck to the frame of the truck above the wheel rim of the spare tire under the bed. You have to take the tire off to get to it and then it's not noticeable unless you're looking for it." Willie Gardner appears pleased to present this information to his wife.

"Are you saying I have to take the spare tire off to get Bel out of the camper?"

"That would give you the confidence to do it alone if you ever have to."

She wants to smack him, she really does.

"But my keys are in the ignition," Willie continues in that infuriating voice. "I'm surprised you didn't notice them hanging there. When you're done, put them back in the ignition so we know where they are. Remember now, you want the small silver one right next to the ignition key. I used the same system on my key ring as on yours." For a second Willie pauses. "No, Spider. I came here to run my buggy and that's what I'm going to do. Let's get Mike's rig off his trailer."

§

It's quiet now inside the camper and Sheri pauses before unlocking the door. Her children, she realizes, have grown accustomed to their confinement. Willie has conceived a master stroke. He's reduced the complexities of parenthood to a single silver key. Keep them in there! Pass them food on a tray under the door. No sugar, no stimulants. Control everything. No music later than the big band era. For entertainment the novels of Dickens and radio shows from the 30s.

When Sheri finally opens the door Bel lunges out stumbling in the sand.

"Blaahh! He is so disgusting, *I'm* going to puke." She points back toward the camper, refusing to look.

On the bed up in the loft Brad has turned a pale green. His breakfast eggs, sausage, orange juice, bits of toast all seasoned with a rich scattering of partially crushed M&Ms are pooled on the spread next to his head. He still has his bush hat on. His walkie-talkie lies abandoned beside him.

Sheri cannot get him to move. When she puts her hand on his ankle he kicks it away.

Willie Gardner is called to the scene. Bel informs him that he drove like an idiot. It was like being up in a tree during a storm. A tornado maybe.

"Brad," Willie says. "You need to get up."

Bradley moans.

"Son, this is not the way a man behaves. You need to get out of the camper so your mother can clean this up."

"Why should she clean it up?" Bel announces from outside. "You're the one drove like a maniac!"

"I need to get going," Willie says in confidence to his wife. "The boys are waiting."

"Great. So, you intend to sleep in this?"

Her husband studies the situation. "He'll feel better in a few minutes. Nobody likes to lie in their own vomit. Once he's out of there you can clean it up in no time. There's not much."

"It's soaking in!"

"Why should she clean it up? Did she drive?"

"Bel," Sheri says.

"Well," Bel says.

Willie and Sheri Gardner look at their son, his face buried in the bedspread, his knees drawn up to his chest. A thought is born that Sheri tries her best to push away. But it doesn't go away. It spreads malignantly inside her, rising dark and unwelcome to the surface. This is your son, the thought announces. This is who he is. Being miserable, moaning and lying next to his own puke; our son is expressing his very essence.

But Willie does not have time to stand around contemplating their youngest born. The Boys are waiting, ready to go. He grabs up the four corners of the bedspread, makes a huge bundle of kid, puke, pillows and spread and heads for the door.

"Willie! Wait! Willie, be careful!"

Backing to a safe distance Bel gives her assessment: "You are crazy! You know that?"

Willie sets the bundle on the floor near the door. He hops down, grasps the bundle again, swings it out and drops it in the sand. A loud groan emerges from inside, a kicking of feet. Freed from the bedding Brad staggers off a few steps before dropping down in the sand.

Belinda has fallen silent, hand over her mouth. Sheri grips the doorframe as if experiencing an earthquake. Good Wife Dot, her husband Spider Webb and Needy Mike the Recently Jilted are pointedly not watching.

Willie tears off the pillow cases, grabs up the bedspread and gives it a good shake. The walkie-talkie goes flying, bits of vomit hurtle off. He carries the spread and pillow cases to the front of the truck and drapes them across the hood; he grabs a cannister of water and pours the contents across the stains.

"All right, everything's clean," he says to the three of them. "And the hood's still warm from the engine. Spread'll be dry in no time. But be careful. The wind comes up and that spread falls wet in the sand we'll have a mess."

"Dad, get my bike down."

"Son, if you want your bike, you'll have to get it yourself. The boys are waiting. I got to get my buggy off."

Willie Gardner leaves them on the little mound of beach like a random collection of shells and kelp bulbs above the pounding surf and below the crumbling bluff. Belinda fishes the tape player from the pouch on her sweatshirt and turns it on. Bradley finishes the water Sheri has given him. He drops the glass in the sand and lies down beside it. Sheri picks up the glass and wipes it off. Her lips taste of salt. They are still there when the three men roar off in their buggies. They appear stunned, as if they miss Willie already.

§

Good Wife Dot informs Sheri that her husband Willie Gardner is a saint. Sheri is making the first pot of coffee in the new camper.

"If he's not helping somebody out of a jam, he's building a beautiful thing like this."

As Sheri sets out the cups she contemplates the idea that her husband is a saint. She imagines Willie with a tiny halo around his burry head. She pictures white wings emerging from his freckled back. The halo doesn't work, but the wings are okay. He's always flying out the door, that's the sense she has of him.

"Did he tell you what he did for my parents a couple of weeks ago? The flat tire out on Newburg Road?"

"I don't think so."

"That is so like him! Well, they were all gussied up on their way to Ross Thompson's funeral when they had a flat. Running late, as per usual. Dad was trying to figure out what to do when Willie showed up pulling the backhoe. No sooner did he see the problem than he jumped out of the truck and had that tire changed in no time. Dad said he couldn't have stopped him if he'd wanted to. Wouldn't take a penny. Gave that little salute like he does and sent them on their way."

"Answered their prayers," says the wife of Willie Gardner.

"And just look at this! You are so lucky, Sheri. Last year the remodeled bathroom and now this. And everything first class. You know, when you buy these units off the lot you have problems. They look good but the parts are cheap and the guys that bang 'em together...well, it's an assembly line. Minimum wage, if that. Illegal immigrants, probably. Then they give you a warranty that reads good but just try and get something out of them. Remember our water heater? First the thermostat was all screwed up. Then it started leaking. I spent hours on the phone just trying to get past the busy signal. Finally, Spider had to tear it out himself and replace the tank and the fittings. He was ready to kill someone."

"Did he?" Bel is sitting in the sun leaning against the doorframe. She looks up at Dot, her face the picture of innocence.

"What, hon?"

"Kill them."

Dot looks at Sheri. Sheri says, "Bel, what kind of question is that?"

"Well, he wanted to beat up Rod Blessing, didn't he?"

"It was a figure of speech, Bel," Sheri says.

"Whatever." Bel drops onto the sand, and then she's gone.

The mother of Belinda Gardner is embarrassed. She pours their coffee and sits down across from Dot.

"My children are driving me bananas."

"Oh no!" Dot exclaims. "I understand perfectly. Bel was upset by what Spider said. And Spider was upset too. I think he feels sorry for Mike, beings Mike has such bad luck with women. No, it's not Bel's fault. You shouldn't feel bad about that."

Through the open door Sheri can see her daughter walking away. Bel has removed her sweatshirt and is dragging it along beside her, one sleeve trailing in the sand. She is practicing, to good effect, her ass-swaying walk.

§

"Mom! Mom!" Sheri Gardner's son has great faith in the power of his voice. Instead of coming to where you are, he goes to where he wants you to be and yells. This time it's the front of the truck.

Sheri has yet to enjoy her first sip of coffee. If she were home now, she thinks, she'd be back from exercise class and taking twenty minutes in the tub. The TV would be on and she'd have a cup of coffee in her hand. The warmth would be exquisite.

The hot tub is what Willie did the winter before after Sheri insisted he resign as fire chief so he could spend more time with his family. Remodeled the bathroom. Extended the outer wall and put in a spa. You can open the sliding glass doors and be pretty much outdoors or you can close them up and feel like you're in the house. Everyone says it's fantastic the job he did.

"Mom! Mom! Help me get my bike down!"

Dot starts to get up saying, "Stay right where you are. I'll help him. The poor kid. I suffer from motion sickness and I know what it's like."

"No, I'll get it."

Sheri finds Brad munching on a candy bar. In a manner she has never fully understood, her son manages to maintain a remarkable stockpile of candy.

"Where's my helmet?"

"Where'd you put it?'

"Dad put it somewhere."

"Have you looked for it?"

"No," Brad says, annoyed at the absurdity of her question. "How can I look for it if I don't know where he put it?"

They disconnect the bike and lower it to the sand. Sheri finds the helmet and brings it back.

"Did you bring the gas?" Brad rests the remains of the candy bar on the seat while he pulls on the helmet. "Get the little can. The one with the oil mixed in. Don't get the wrong can. You can ruin the engine with the wrong gas."

"Where you going?" Sheri asks, pouring the gasoline.

"Out there." He motions vaguely.

"Where's that?"

"Along the beach, I don't know."

"Well, stay out of the water."

"Duh. You think it's a submarine? It's a bike, Mom."

"Stay away from the water, that's all. There's killer waves that come up suddenly. Don't go too far and be back soon. And pick that up."

Brad picks up the candy bar wrapper and hands it to his mother.

"You want something to eat before you go?"

"I'm all right."

"I can make you a sandwich to take along."

"Naw, I'll be back." Her son is sitting on the bike now. He kicks it on. The noise is high-pitched and ugly. Then he yells something that shocks them both.

"Thanks, Mom." Then he, too, is gone, his rear tire weaving in the sand.

§

Willie, Needy Mike and Spider Webb roar into camp about one expecting lunch. Good Wife Dot and Sheri set out sandwiches, potato chips and dip. Spider produces a six pack of beer that they pass around. To the apparent delight of Willie and Spider, Needy Mike has a problem with the choke on his buggy. They have to figure out a way to fix it without much equipment and no parts. So they set their sandwiches and beers on rocks and seats and tinker and curse and eat their sandwiches and drink their beers and toss the bag of chips back and forth and find scraps of wire and piece the damn thing together so it'll run till they get back to town. Needy Mike drinks his beer and watches from a nearby rock.

Bel does not return. Neither does Brad. Sheri is worried but Willie says there's no reason to worry. It's the middle of the day, a nice day, and besides the boys are ready to roll. He doesn't want to spend the afternoon looking for the kids when they've only been gone an hour or two. He and the boys are heading toward the mouth of Lost River and if he sees the kids he'll check on them. Then Willie Gardner and the boys roar off.

Dot and Sheri clean up the lunch. They get out the pup tents and set them up for Bel and Brad. Then they sit in the sun and read romance novels and talk about Linda and Needy Mike. When the sun goes down a wind comes up and it gets even colder. And the kids aren't back.

The women set out great slabs of beef. They start the charcoal and season the potatoes and wrap them in foil. In the little trailer that belongs to Spider and his Good Wife they have a glass of wine. Dot tries with all the earnestness she can muster to convince Sheri that the kids are fine, and of course it doesn't work. Sheri's imagination is racing and it seems to her that of all the possible things that could have happened, most of them are bad.

"And there's another thing," she tells Dot. "My family has moved to someplace far away. That's how it feels. Not some physical place. But someplace away and they're living their lives in that place and I'm not there with them. I'm at the edge of their lives, just at the edge."

Dot is so earnest now she looks like she's going to cry. She says, no, that Sheri is at the very center.

But Sheri says it doesn't seem that way to her. "If somehow you could measure my family, and then you measured it again, this time with me not there, the two numbers would be about the same. I don't matter. The numbers would be the same with me or without me. That's what it feels like."

Dot has tears in her eyes and she says, no, that's not true.

Sheri says it seems true to her. "And I don't know how it happened because I married Willie and I had those children and I don't understand how I ended up so far away."

Now Sheri has tears in her eyes too and she feels kind of stupid and Dot is hugging her and getting them both some tissues and telling her how the kids love her and how Willie just adores her and how he talks about her all the time. Sheri, the wife of Willie Gardner, wipes her eyes and pours herself some more wine.

That's when Brad bursts through the door. He staggers across the floor and falls on the couch. The boy is sunburned and his clothes hang precariously about him. The walkie-talkie dangles from his wrist and sand pours from his pants and shoes all over the floor and couch. His helmet lands on the floor with a dull thud and rattles back and forth for a moment, the chinstraps flopping.

"God," he moans, "I've been walking for years!"

"Bradley, where have you been?"

"Walking. What'd I just say? Walking." Another moan. "God, I'm starved. My bike broke down miles from here, just miles."

"Of course you are!" Dot grabs chips and dip and sandwich makings and a can of soda and sets them all before Brad who accepts them without a word of appreciation.

"Where's Dad, he'll have to get it."

"You left your bike out there?" Sheri is on her knees scraping sand off the floor with her fingers while Dot is saying Sheri doesn't have to do that, that she could sweep it out later. "Where's your bike, Bradley?"

"It's by a rock."

"By a rock? What rock? You didn't push it back?"

"Mom, have you walked in sand for miles? Have you tried pushing a mini-bike through heavy sand? No, I guess not. You're lucky I wasn't killed. There's animals out there. There's rattlesnakes in the driftwood. I had to walk in the dark. Dad'll have to go find it."

Sheri remembers that moment earlier in the day when her son thanked her. She takes his shoes off and rubs the sand off his socks and into one of his shoes. She turns down his cuffs and tries to get the sand out of the cuffs and into the shoe so she can take the whole mess outside. Dot brings Bradley a second root beer.

"Well, he's not back," Sheri tells her son. "Belinda either."

"She's with Stu Elway."

Sheri gasps. "Stu Elway? Isn't he out of high school? He must be eighteen or nineteen."

"Nineteen," Dot says, her voice a church-like whisper, her head nodding slowly. "He's the same age as my little brother Gary."

"Guy's a jerk. He looked at my bike like three seconds. Said it couldn't be fixed. Wouldn't give me a ride neither. Bel wanted him to, too."

"Bradley, where was this?"

"Where'd I say? Miles from here. He's got this creepy old motorcycle claims he's gonna restore. Right. Guy can't fix my throttle cable and he's gonna restore a motorcycle? Right."

Sheri seems to have fallen into a state of paralysis. Dot takes Brad's shoe out of her hand, carries it to the door and dumps the sand outside. Then she hands Sheri her glass of wine.

§

They cook their steaks standing in the dark night with the surf hissing and a cold damp wind blowing along the shoreline like some malevolent force searching out a weak spirit. Sheri bounces up and down, her neck compressed into her shoulders, her hands squeezed under her armpits, saying to Good Wife Dot, "And this is supposed to be fun? Is there a woman in the whole world who thinks camping is fun? This is not fun. This is so third-world! This is women in caves chewing on hides!"

They have just started to eat when they see the first flash of headlights wavering along the shoreline. The lights are set high on the roll bar and the noise is ominous causing Sheri to imagine for a moment some menacing military vehicle coming toward them. But of course it's not some menacing military vehicle. It's just Willie Gardner driving his beach buggy across the hard wet sand, wearing his CAT cap, a flannel shirt unbuttoned over his T-shirt, moving slow and loud, driving it like a tractor.

He has Spider Webb's broken down buggy secured behind his with a rope, and tied behind the Spider's rig with another rope is the buggy of Needy Mike the Recently Jilted who is by now solemnly drunk and soundly asleep behind the wheel. The knots on the ropes have been elegantly tied by the scout master and former Eagle Scout. Stuffed in the back of Spider's rig are the best parts of a poached deer which had the misfortune of getting within range of the carbine Spider always keeps stashed on his buggy. Lashed to the back of Needy Mike's rig is the mini-bike left by the rock, and standing on the frame steering Mike's buggy is Bel Gardner, the true daughter of Captain Willie Gardner, her cassette player at full volume, singing along at the top of her lungs.

Willie pulls the caravan into camp. He honks the horn, gives that little salute he likes to give and kills the engine.

Dot runs to get beers for the travelers and Sheri feels something powerful rise up inside her. It comes from the involuntary part, the part she has no control over, the part that tells her toenails to grow and her blood to flow, the part that sets her stomach to work when gobs of burrito are heading its way. It's a feeling of warmth and admiration, of gratitude and desire. It is unwanted, it really is, and it is so damned delicious.

Her meal abandoned, Sheri pulls the hood of the sweatshirt over her head. She slips her hands up inside the sleeves, grabs the remaining steaks and heads for the door. If she doesn't get out there quick she knows full well that Willie will hop off that buggy and cook the damn things himself.

BLACK FAIRLANE

Memories cluster, images come in strands trailing blips of emotion. Impressions of Susan. I feel a certain eagerness, agitation, a sense, perhaps, of urgency...

§

I turned nineteen a long time ago, on February 3rd, 1959 to be exact. Which was the same day a small plane crashed in Iowa killing the pilot and three musicians: Buddy Holly, Ritchie Valens and J.P. Richards, better known as the Big Bopper. They were heading up the Winter Dance Party tour and had been scheduled to perform in Peoria two days later. I had purchased a ticket weeks before and the show went on without the stars. It was a mournful evening in the theater, the Crickets up there singing and strumming without Buddy. The concert would have been an ideal occasion for a date, but I was a sister-less mama's boy, and, at nineteen, girls had an allure that both obsessed and paralyzed me. So I went with my friend Andrew Barnes and Thomas, his older brother.

Thomas worked in the foundry at Caterpillar, and Andrew had recently gotten on with the railroad as a fireman. By that February, I had already learned that business college did not appeal to me, or me to it, which is saying the same thing I guess, So I dropped out, an act that greatly distressed my mother, who had herself graduated from the business college and worked in a local bank.

I was stocking shelves part time at a local market and picking up odd jobs here and there, telling my worried mother over breakfast that I would start college in the fall. This was a promise she feared I might not keep, or if I did, not succeed at. My performance in high school had done little to encourage her. My father, who had left school after eighth grade, worked in the assembly line of a factory. Such was the fate shared by most of the men and boys in our town, and the one my mother feared awaited me.

The railroad job gave Andrew a chance to pursue a dream he had had all through high school: he purchased an immaculate, low mileage 1957 Ford Fairlane convertible off a lot in a town near our own.

I can still picture him in the library back when we were sophomores: its study hall, he's a scrawny kid hunched over a notebook sketching a car.

So pronounced was this desire Andrew had, that when he finally bought the Fairlane his dad surrendered the family garage to his youngest son so the boy's prized possession could be kept safely out of the elements. And his mom carefully laundered the white terrycloth towels Andrew had purchased so he could properly wash, polish and wipe down his newly acquired possession.

In August of that year, Andrew and I took the Fairlane up to Devil's Lake, Wisconsin for a weekend of camping. We had been there the year before with Thomas and we'd been talking about going back all summer. We left on a Friday afternoon as soon as Andrew clocked out. Fueled by candy bars, vending machine coffee and the heavy rhythms blasting from the AM radio, we drove north for seven hours, the wind wild in our hair, the humid air cooling in the dips of the road as the night came on.

It was well after midnight when we arrived the lake and the next morning we drove straight to the Chateau. Everyone called it the Chateau, but the building was not a castle or a country estate as the word implies. I remember a single-story, nondescript structure set beside the north shore of the lake. Outside you could rent a rowboat or canoe. The interior was woody, the floors and walls, the overhead beams, the gouged and initialed booths along the walls. There was a jukebox and a dance floor, a tiny store that sold food, charcoal and other camping supplies, and a counter where you could order sodas, hot dogs and hamburgers. (Adults could purchase beer, a privilege that allowed them to sit on the "adult" side of the dance floor, the side with the best view of the lake.) We young people were drawn to the Chateau because it offered the possibility of what gamblers call "action," that is, the opportunity to pursue your desires in the face of risk.

When we stepped inside the Chateau that Saturday morning, seeing how familiar it looked, hearing the music coming from the jukebox, catching the scent of the place, I felt as if we had come home, as if, seeing us, everyone should stand and welcome us back. That was absurd, of course. But that was the feeling.

We bought quarts of milk and some of those little powdered donuts that came in a blue box with a plastic window, the donuts squeezed in so tightly that when you freed them they came out more square than round. We were eagerly breaking our fast, so giddy to be back at the lake, back in the Chateau, that we didn't notice the three girls until they had stopped and were standing at the edge of our booth, staring down on us as if we were a pair of odd specimens in a museum display case.

The two of us freeze, Andrew's eyes meeting mine.

Then one of the girls, it was the one who turned out to be Lorna, said, "Look at those donuts, girls! I just love those little donuts."

So, of course, we invited them to join us.

Of the three girls, I thought Lorna the most intriguing. For one thing, as we learned a few minutes later, she was Jewish. This might sound impossible today, but until that moment Andrew and I had never in our lives met a person we knew to be Jewish. In our high school there were town kids and farm kids, Protestant kids and Catholic kids, but everyone was Caucasian, Christian, heterosexual (or in the dark of night prayed they were) and spoke English as their first and only language.

Another thing about Lorna, she always had a deck of cards in her hands. If we were sitting in the Chateau or in the little restaurant that was down the street from their cabin, she'd deal some cards out on the table and play solitaire while the five of us talked. Or maybe she'd look over at you with her green eyes and if you nodded she'd divide the deck and the two of you would play war while the conversation continued. She was very protective of her cards. When the powdered sugar began to land in flurries on the table, she borrowed a cloth from the soda counter and carefully wiped it clean.

Peaches was the cutest of the three in my mind: a short fleshy blonde with thick red lips and dimples that flashed on and off as if lit in some way. She carried a sketchpad and a packet of pencils wherever she went. "Don't move," she would demand, and pinching her lips tightly, would sketch your profile, or the backside of your hand, or the sunglasses you had just set on the table.

The third girl, Susan, might have been thought plain. She was thin, her brown hair dutiful. Acne corroded her face which appeared scrubbed, picked upon and pasted over as if it were a work in progress. But she was also mysterious, and, I later realized, she was probably as shy around boys as I was around girls. Peaches said that she loved drawing Susan's eyes because they were the prettiest eyes she had ever seen. She described them as being "hazel," a description that didn't make a lot of sense to me. I saw flecks of green and brown. But what I noticed about Susan's eyes was an alert stillness. You got the impression she could look into your soul and see what was there.

They were seventeen, and they came from Madison or some town near there. They attended the same high school and they had arrived at the lake with Susan's parents but they had their own cabin on the north shore. It was a big deal for the girls because Susan's parents were staying at a different place entirely and the girls were free to stay out late, sleep in, cook what they wanted, do in fact whatever it was they chose to do.

After we had eaten most of the donuts Susan asked, "Can you boys recount for us how you came to spend the night sleeping in a car?" In my memory, that is exactly the way Susan talked. As if in her other life, that is her interior life, she was Jane Austin's younger sister.

"Well, it is a nice car," Andrew said, a hint defensive.

"Yeah, it is," I said. "A Ford Fairlane convertible. Black with a white top, red interior, whitewalls all around. Almost new, a '57 model."

Finding my description inadequate, Andrew threw in: "It's got a V-8 under the hood. Two-hundred-seventy horses."

The girls went silent for a moment, their eyes squinting. This practice they had, which I would become very familiar with in the coming days, was somewhat eerie. It was if they had the ability to exchange thoughts back and forth, hold a telepathic discussion about how they should respond to the information they had just received, and who would speak on their behalf.

Finally Susan said, "Well, it seems to me if you have a car that nice you wouldn't want people using it as a bedroom." The other girls nodded their heads in agreement.

Andrew's face got even rosier than usual. "Well, we brought a pup tent. But it was after midnight when we got here."

Susan and Peaches smiled in unison and Peaches said, "So you arrived at the lake too late to put up your tent."

"We drove through the camping area on the south shore but it was real dark and real quiet. Everyone was sleeping."

"So you didn't want to disturb the other campers by pounding in tent stakes after midnight," Susan said, nodding her head eagerly as if to accentuate her appreciation of what she took to be our good manners.

"Or slamming car doors," Peaches added. "That was nice of you."

"And we didn't have a permit either," I said. "So we found a little gravel road just outside the park. We parked under a big old tree and went to sleep."

"Well, we tried to sleep," Andrew interjected, laughing suddenly. "But then we got bushwhacked."

I remembered then. "Yeah! We did! We got bushwhacked!"

The girls went into that silent thinking place again. Then Lorna spoke, pausing with her cards, "Bushwhacked? That's not a word we know. Where are you boys from anyway?"

"It must be a great distance, Lorna," Susan suggested, "to have arrived after midnight."

"And speaking such a strange language," Lorna added, placing the seven of hearts on the eight of clubs.

Now Andrew and I were confused. "You know, bushwhacked! Like some couple is parked down a road at night, some make-out place, okay, and you sneak up with flashlights and start banging on the hood and fenders. Bushwhacking!"

Peaches frowned, her red lips puckered: "That sounds cruel."

"It does," Susan agreed. "And crude."

"Sounds hillbillyish to me," Lorna said. "Where *are* you boys from anyway?"

"We didn't do it. They did it to us!"

Susan had borrowed my pocketknife and she was carefully dividing the last donut into five tiny pieces which she carefully set out in a row on top of the empty box. It had begun to rain. We could see the front moving like a screen across the lake.

"It all makes sense now," Susan said, wiping the blade and handing the knife back to me.

"Well, sort of, Susan" Lorna replied. "We still don't really know where these boys are from, or why they speak this strange language or what they're doing here at the lake on a Saturday morning eating donuts in the Chateau."

"Well, not just eating their donuts, Lorna, sharing them." Susan smiled at us.

"I'm just hoping they don't do that cruel sort of thing themselves," Peaches said. She bit down on her lower lip and looked at me intently as if trying to read my mind.

But then Andrew saved the day. Sounding just like a boy who would own a black '57 Ford Fairlane convertible even though the monthly payments ate up about ninety percent of his take-home pay, he made a pronouncement: "Tim and me, we'd rather be the ones doing the parking than the ones doing the bushwhacking."

The girls considered this in silence and then Lorna said, "Would someone please spin a few platters?"

She takes up her cards and shuffles them skillfully. "Seven Up?" She looks across the table at Andrew.

"I'm not thirsty."

"It's a card game, silly. Here, let me show you."

§

The rain stopped before noon and the clouds broke up, though for a while tufts of them still pawed at the tops of the bluffs. Andrew and I found a campsite and pitched our tent. We met the girls at their cabin where they offered us Swiss cheese sandwiches enlivened with thick smears of yellow mustard. Then we set out together to climb the bluff on the lake's east side.

After a half hour of climbing we arrived at a point where rows of tree-covered bluff lines were visible to the east. To the west, the lake lay below us. We came upon a steep quartzite face and Lorna challenged us to climb it. After searching around she finally found the best ascent and led us to the top. "She's our brave one," Susan whispered to me.

It was pleasant sitting on the broad relatively flat surface, the stone warm in the sun, a few lingering clouds puffy along the horizon. We must have stayed an hour or more on that rock. Lorna taught Andrew to play Kaluki. Peaches tried to "rat" some of my hair and ended up tying it with a pale blue bow. Susan opened her little book of Edna St. Vincent Millay's sonnets and read to us while on the lake below a water skier carved graceful white arcs in the blue water.

"There's my car!" Andrew is shouting from the precipice.

It was true. Standing at the edge you could see the white canvas top just visible through the trees.

Susan nudged my shoulder and nodded toward Andrew. The three girls were smiling at me as if they are sharing my thought about Andrew (or was it *our* thought?), the thought that he had just realized maybe for the first time that he, Andrew Barnes, could actually be the owner of such a marvelous car.

§

The girls were spending a full week at the cabin. Andrew and I had only three days, and we spent all the time we could with them. Andrew loved driving his Fairlane and the girls loved going for rides. Lorna always sat up front while Susan, Peaches and I shared the back. To watch the road we had to peer past the fuzzy black dice that dangled from the rearview mirror.

Andrew had fastened a knob on the steering wheel so he could steer with one casual hand. Except when parking he preferred to have just a finger or two resting on the knob, his left elbow jutting out the open window while the wind tangled the girls' hair, blowing it forward over their faces.

Lorna was in charge of the radio, and she searched the dial for Buddy Holly songs, his tragic death having enlivened his music in some indefinable way. (How impressed the girls were that we had *almost* seen him.) After a ride they would wash their hair, the five of us sitting on the steps of their cabin as they combed it out; the smells of shampoo and damp hair drying in the sun.

Sunday we went horseback riding. On Monday Andrew removed some of the white, carefully-laundered, terrycloth towels from the pinkish pillowcase where he kept them safe in the trunk, and the five us washed and waxed the Fairlane.

Peaches is on her rump buffing a whitewall, legs crossed, her squinting face reflecting in the hubcap.

Then we drove north to the Dells where we rode the children's rides and browsed through the souvenir shops.

Much of the time we spent at the Chateau. We played endless games of cards, slid multiple quarters into the jukebox and danced to replays of "Peggy Sue" and the Drifters singing, "There goes my Baby." Lorna, having decided my buckskin engineer boots were "so cool," insisted on wearing them when she danced.

Each night, after the Chateau closed at eleven, we drove down the same gravel road where Andrew and I had spent our first night. In the front seat, Andrew and Lorna made out, the radio playing, while in the back the three of us were "best friends ever." We hugged, we laughed, we exchanged a few kisses, but mostly we talked. Susan whispered poetry into my eager ear, her slender fingers brushing my neck, while Peaches confided her troubled history with boys. With her warm thigh pressed ever more tightly against my own, she described mean boys, boorish boys and that one impossible dream boy whose slights and betrayals had inflicted multiple injuries on her tender heart. In my assigned role of friend and attentive listener, waves of lust, guilt and self-pity washed through me, my testicles aching with frustrated desire.

It would be close to three when we finally delivered the girls back to their cabin.

§

On Monday evening we ate at a burger joint in Baraboo. We were all tired and a little sad. Andrew and I planned to leave as early as we could the next morning.

At one point Lorna picked up a long fry. She dipped it in the pool of ketchup, reached across the table and fed it to Andrew. Then we all started doing it, dipping fries in the ketchup and feeding them to one another.

"This is just like communion," Peaches said, chewing thoughtfully.

"Well, it is our last supper," I noted.

"My body, my blood," Susan cried. "How perfect!"

"Susan," Lorna pointed out, "these are French fries. They come from potatoes. That's ketchup. It's made from tomatoes." She looked at me and shook her head.

But then a little later the girls suddenly went quiet. They had slid again into that space of shared silence they seemed capable of entering whenever they chose. Once again it was Susan who spoke.

"We have a proposal to make," she said quite seriously. "But before we say what it is, we want to tell you something."

"Okay?" Andrew and I glanced at each other.

"We want you to know that we would not do this with any other boys."

Andrew and I looked at each other again. "Do what?"

"She's saying that we trust you," Peaches said. "We really trust you." The three of them were nodding their heads.

"Okay?"

"You see," Susan continued, "Lorna tells us that she got drunk once."

"I *did* get drunk once," Lorna insisted. "Really drunk. Sick drunk. The dry heaves, the whole ball of wax."

Susan acknowledged the truth of this. "Yes, Lorna *did* get drunk once. I believe her when she says that."

"So do I," Peaches said, her face pinched as if she could almost experience Lorna's dry heaves.

"But Peaches and I have never gotten drunk."

"I had a little champagne last year at my sister's wedding," Peaches said, "just a couple of sips."

"Not even close," Lorna said.

"No," Peaches admitted "I felt maybe a little tipsy, but I didn't get close to drunk."

"So…" Susan paused.

"So, you want to get drunk?" Andrew asked. "With us?"

"A little drunk," Lorna explained. "Not like last time. Two beers, three at most. You boys have any beer? In your tent maybe?"

"No, but Andrew does have an altered ID. He's used it before."

The girls looked at us.

Andrew leaned back in the booth. He flashed his famous blue-eyed grin and he said: "Ladies, it will be an honor."

§

We parked again at that wide spot at the side of the gravel road. Not directly beneath the big maple this time because a car was already there when we arrived, a Chevy, green and white, a '53 model, maybe a '54. Andrew, who loved to demonstrate his parking skills, maneuvered the Fairlane around and backed it into place so its trunk was facing the trunk of the Chevy maybe twenty feet away.

It had begun to rain softly some time earlier and we had put the top up back in Baraboo. Inside, even with the windows mostly down, it felt hot and muggy. We could hear the rain striking the canvas above our heads.

When Andrew turned off the lights it became very dark, the only illumination coming from the dial of the radio. Behind us, the Chevy was also dark but you could hear music coming faintly from it as well. The cars were like two uninhabited islands set out on a dark sea, each independent of the other, music coming from both.

Andrew had managed to get two six packs of "The Beer that made Milwaukee famous" which were stashed now at Lorna's feet. She found the church key in the glove compartment and handed it to him. Then working in the dark, she broke out five cans. One by one Andrew opened them, the abrupt liquid-sounding rasp as he cut the large triangular hole, the little punch-like scrape as he poked the tiny opening on the opposite side. The smell of beer, heady, illicit and intoxicating filled the car. We were all strangely quiet as he performed this task and solemn as he handed out the cans.

"Cheers," he said at last.

The beer party was ridiculously brief. The five of us were so tired that after a few sips we were saying things like, "Is that your foot or mine?" and then giggling uncontrollably.

Half way through the first can, Peaches, Susan and I were slobbering on each other's shoulders, swearing we would never forget this night or each other. A short time later all of us, or at least the three of us in the backseat, were asleep.

"Oh, oh," I heard Andrew mutter sometime later.

"What?" Lorna asked.

"Cops maybe," Andrew whispered. I became aware then of the sound of car tires moving slowly over gravel. Andrew pulled himself up so he was sitting behind the wheel. Lorna too had begun to stir.

"I don't see any lights," I whispered. My head was on Peaches's lap. She was slumped against the window frame breathing deeply. Susan was leaning on both of us, our arms and legs entangled.

"His lights aren't on," Andrew said quietly.

"That's not a cop car," Lorna said.

"Is it going past?"

"No, it's stopping now."

I lifted Susan slowly and leaned her against the far wall. Then I sat up so I could see past Peaches. The car had stopped a couple of car lengths away. It was all one color, a dark green, blue maybe. Its outline suggested a Pontiac of some sort. For a couple of minutes nothing happened.

"Parkers," I started to say, but then the door on the driver's side opened and a man stepped out. When the interior light came on we could see there was no one else in the car. The man closed the door very gently. Then he began walking stealthily toward the Chevy parked behind us. In his right hand he was carrying something.

That can't be a gun, I thought.

"What?" Susan asked, starting to waken.

"Sshh," Lorna said.

"A what?" Peaches, too, was beginning to move. We were all turning now, trying to see through the rear rain-streaked plastic window. The man reached the Chevy. For a few seconds he just stood there. Then he bent down and peered into the back seat.

"Let's get out of here," Andrew said softly; I heard the jingle of his keys in the ignition.

"No, wait." Lorna stuck her head and shoulders out the passenger side window so she could better see behind us.

The man grabbed the back door and pulled. The door was locked. Then he shouted something I couldn't understand and swinging the object in his hand he shattered the window. There was screaming. The man reached through, opened the door and as the car's interior light came on he leaned inside.

We heard an explosion and Andrew started the engine.

"No!" Lorna yelled. "We can't!"

The man pulled a woman out of the backseat. His free hand held her upper arm and he pushed her backward over the trunk of the car. Her legs flew up, her clothes were half off and hanging about her. She was flailing her arms, screaming and writhing against the man's grip. He slammed the pistol against the side of her face with a backhanded whipping motion.

We heard a thick, sickening, bone-crushing sound as the weapon stuck her.

"Stop that!" Lorna is out of the car. She's running toward them. The man turns and swings his arm.

"Lorna!" Susan and Peaches screamed in unison. They were trying to climb over the seat to get to the door.

We heard a second explosion and Lorna crumpled, a collapsing, sideways, forward fall that caused her to disappear from view. By pushing my head hard against the canvas top I could make out her head and shoulders.

Lorna lay a few feet beyond our car, perhaps ten feet from the man. *I see the flair of her wavy clean-washed hair spread motionless on the ground.*

"No!" "No!" "No!" "No!" all of us were screaming, as if a feverish incantation could somehow refute this moment and revert us back to one before.

I couldn't see the man's face clearly but his posture, his legs half-separated and slightly bowed, his shoulders slumped, his arms hanging useless at his sides, suggested a state of abject wonder, as if some inverse miracle had transpired, as if he had been plucked from one reality and set down in another where he recognized no past, saw no future and had but one act left to perform. With a curious spasmodic motion he raised the pistol. Jamming the barrel into his mouth, he pulled the trigger.

§

The man in the backseat had a bullet wound in his right shoulder. Once he had extracted himself from the car, pulling his jeans up from his calves, his right thumb pressed against the bullet hole, he stood beside the shooter's body repeating, "Well, God damn. Well, I'll be God damn." An almost gleeful quality could be heard in his voice. It was as if he had just seen a whale suddenly breach the surface of the lake, slapping its tail and causing rowboats to flip over in its wake.

Whimpering and holding her face, the woman on the trunk slid off the back and set herself hard on the bumper as if she were a third-grader scolded and ordered to sit in the corner.

Lorna's body is warm, pliable and unhelpful as we turn her. She was silent as only the dead are silent, uncooperative in that way that only the dead can be uncooperative.

For a short while Susan and Peaches stumbled in ragged circles screaming in the night at the tops of their registers. Then as if mutually summoned they rushed back to Lorna's body, and kneeling on either side began kissing her face and hands. They straightened her limbs and clothing as if setting her out for a visitation. Peaches began to comb Lorna's hair, the two girls whimpering as they worked. As their tears splashed down onto Lorna's face, Susan carefully wiped them off with the side of her little finger.

Andrew and I staggered about, babbled meaninglessly at each other in sobs and mutters and then seeing the girls we fell silent, excluded and in awe.

The rain continued to fall in drops large and small, working its way through the tree's many leaves and branches to strike softly on rock and weed, on canvas, fender and flesh.

Time, we eventually realized, would never start again until somebody did something. So Andrew got into the Fairlane and drove down the road to the nearest occupied structure and telephoned the law.

§

At the courthouse where they told us to go after the deputies and ambulances had come and gone, the four of us sat on a bench in a corridor, and one by one we were called into the office. The corridor was on the second floor of a building that was old even then.

At one end was the courtroom, and at the other the office of the county sheriff. At that hour the courtroom was closed, the milk-glass windows dark in the double doors. Two janitors were working down near the doors. The younger one, a white boy who was about the same age as Andrew and I, did the mopping while an older African-American man ran the buffer. The buffer rumbled, the wheeled water bucket rattled as it was moved and the wet mop made a soft slapping sound when it landed on the tiled floor.

Peaches came out of the office and said "I just told them everything that happened." Then she dropped onto the bench and started to cry again.

While Susan was in the office her parents arrived, running up the stairs their breaths rasping. Peaches jumped up and fell into their arms. Andrew and I got up too but the parents did not know us, nor we them. It felt awkward standing there so we sat back down. The parents wore white windbreakers and matching pale-blue Bermuda shorts with white socks and tennis shoes. The hair on the man's legs was a shade lighter than his richly tanned skin. Andrew's dad and mine were both blue-color working men. Neither of us had ever seen our fathers wear shorts or tennis shoes or, for that matter, white windbreakers, much less our moms. Susan's parents looked like they'd just stepped off a sailboat. Our parents didn't sail or play golf or attend cocktail parties. These people, I thought, probably did all three.

When Susan came out the four of them stood in the middle of the corridor sobbing and clinging to each other as I was called inside.

The deputy was the same one who had arrived first after Andrew's call. On his desk the day calendar was still open to Monday but it was Tuesday now according to the clock ticking on the wall behind him. He had me sit down. "Tell me everything," he said.

§

When I came out of the office Andrew sat alone on the bench. The two janitors continued to mop and buff the corridor as if we weren't there.

"The girls?"

"They left," Andrew said.

"No, wait, I need…. I have to see them."

"I know. They just took them away."

I sat down. It felt as if their leaving had ripped something out of me. Andrew and I were still on the bench when Susan's father came back up the stairs.

"You boys stay there until I get back," he ordered, moving toward the office door. "I want to talk to you."

"Where are the girls?"

"You'll have nothing more to do with the girls," he said. Then stopping, he turned and faced us directly. "I know what you boys were after. I know what you had in mind!" He smelled of cologne and gin.

"What? We…"

"If you hadn't gotten them drunk…."

Just then, Susan came running up the stairs followed by Peaches and Susan's mother.

"Dad…"

"Go back to the car, Susan. All of you, wait in the car, I mean it. Gladys, will you please…?"

The girls looked at us as if across a chasm. Then they turned and followed Susan's mother down the stairs. That was the last time Andrew and I would ever see them, though at that moment we didn't know it.

"I'm the one who has to call Lorna's parents!" Susan's father shouted at us. "Do you have any idea what that's going to be like?"

With his head down, as if determined not to see or hear anything, the African-American man continued to operate the buffer. But his young assistant had stopped mopping. He turned to look at us, leaning on the mop handle. The door to the sheriff's office opened then and the officer who had taken our statements stepped into the corridor.

"Sir, you can make that call from in here." And then to us, "You boys are free to go. I think you should leave now."

Outside it was raining harder. All the cars were dark and we had no idea which one the girls were in.

Early in the morning, with our sodden tent and damp bedrolls thrown in the trunk, Andrew and I drove to the girls' cabin. The door was unlocked but their things were gone and there was no sign of them, not there, not at the Chateau, not anywhere else we could think to look. We were two hundred and fifty miles from the railroad yard where Andrew had to clock in by two that afternoon. And I had promised a neighbor that I would paint his garage before the weekend.

§

In a sense the bullet that killed Lorna had entered Andrew as well. In the weeks and months that followed he came to believe that his future had been destroyed. Had that gun not been fired he would have learned Lorna's last name. He would have obtained her address and phone number. He would have written and called her regularly. He would have traveled to see her. They would have fallen in love, become engaged and gotten married. None of that was now possible.

I started college early that September, but in Andrew's world there existed only two things that connected him to Lorna: the black Fairlane and me. No one else could possibly understand him. Getting off work he would drive two hours, arrive at my dorm with a six pack of beer on the seat beside him.

Littered with work boots, scarves and jackets, with empty beer cans, burger wrappers and escaped fries, the Fairlane had become a sort of midden that revealed Andrew's tormented life. He would drive us somewhere private where we could sit in the car and talk. He swore that he had seen Lorna once. He had come out of a movie, he told me, and he saw her walking in the crowd in front of him. He ran to catch up with her but she disappeared. It wasn't mistaken identity, he insisted. She had been there and she had disappeared. Mornings he would wake with the taste of her lips on his own. Once, sitting on a bar stool, he smelled Lorna's shampoo. The smell was overwhelming and unmistakable, causing him to spin on the stool and nearly fall off. All of this needed to be gone over, picked at.

After a couple of beers his mind would return to the scene of the murder. Why hadn't he driven us out of there when he wanted to? All he had to do was turn the key in the ignition. The sound of the engine alone might have frightened the shooter and prevented the whole thing. But failing that he had been sitting right next to Lorna, his skin touching hers. Why hadn't he grabbed her when she opened the door? He could have prevented it. He could have saved her life and saving hers have saved his own.

I didn't begrudge Andrew these visits though they stole valuable study time. I needed solace almost as much as he. Back at the dorm and flat from the beer, I would lie on my bed, worried about him driving home alone.

My dad used to say that if you want to solve a problem, you first need to loosen the knot. Andrew needed to loosen the knot, but instead he impregnated a young woman named Rose that winter. Shy Rose, pale with wispy blond hair and averted eyes. I attended the ceremony; it wasn't really a wedding, possessing as it did more duty than celebration. The following fall, my sophomore year, they had the child. By the time I graduated and moved west, he and Rose had a second child, another boy. My friend Andrew was now twenty pounds heavier. He and the shy Rose had two pale children and a mountain of bills. Andrew sold the Fairlane. He bought a much-used '56 Plymouth sedan with a dented metal sun visor that protruded out over the windshield like an ugly toenail in need of a trim.

§

Night has come bringing thoughts of Susan. Not Susan then; Susan now. Her eightieth birthday has passed, or soon will. Long gone is the tormenting acne; gone too her desire-fueled fear of boys—when she whispered poems into my ear, her fingers would touch my neck with an urgent, hesitant delicacy. I picture her lying fully awake, alone in a room as dark as mine. Sensations cluster about us. They mix and blend. They pass through our minds in strands, through her mind and through mine. We are at peace; the story is told.

BACKSEAT CONVERSATION

Rita pushed herself away, panting. She wanted to wait until their big day. Anthony disagreed. Sooner was better for him. Right now, in fact, was just right.

"Hearts stop," he implored, "cars crash. We have this night together. The cake is fresh from the oven, warm and ready. Let's taste it!"

Rita giggled. "Now you're talking about dessert, but first we must eat our vegetables. You know that."

Then, humming a little tune known only to her, she placed a finger on the steamed up window and traced a heart.

Anthony groaned. He chose to draw a cross.

PENSION ALHAMBRA

Frieda's mother died just before dawn on a cold morning in March, 1982. They shared a bedroom and Frieda was up twice during the night to give Erna her medicine and to help her to the toilet. The old woman cursed the cold and spilled a glass of water on her gown so it had to be changed. There had been worse nights in the preceding four months, but on this morning she was gone.

The following night Frieda had a dream in which a collar heavy and tight against her throat broke loose and fell away. Suddenly, she was in Salzburg walking through the Mirabell Gardens. It was late afternoon, the time it used to be when years before she had walked in the garden coming home from work. Somewhere, a sprinkler came on. She could hear water striking marble statuary, smell it meeting the earth. Then she woke. The room was dark and she was shivering, though she wasn't cold, and just why she was shivering she could not say.

The family establishment had been given the name Pension Alhambra by her father. As a child she would ask her mother why he had chosen such a romantic name for a village pension located in the middle of Austria. "Because he was a blockhead," her mother had once said. Another time Frieda was told, "Stop with the foolish questions." Her mother was of the generation that bridged the wars. Born during the first and widowed by the second, she fit well with those hard years after the fall of the Third Reich. An intelligent, resourceful woman, the times had scrubbed Erna clean of sentiment; in her mind nostalgia was a blemish to be rubbed away, as unwanted as a stain on the floor or a patina on the brass lamps in the hallway.

Still, the name resonated in Frieda's mind with the few memories she had of her father. Sensations, they were, more than memories. She had retained no incidents or physical features, just an expansiveness, a largeness that was at the same time light, and a rolling sensation that she—suspecting herself all the while—associated with laughter. He had changed the name when he bought and remodeled the pension, her mother had told her that. It had been called The Lubeck after Lubeckstrasse, the street it fronted, a narrow road that followed the river and entered the village from the east. Had he for some reason resented that import from the north of Germany? But why Alhambra? There was no indication he had ever traveled, at least not until he entered the military and learned to fly. Perhaps he was ironic, naming a simple pension after a palace, or a fool, a blockhead, as her mother had said. At the very least, Frieda decided, the name Alhambra suggested in her father an appreciation for the different, the novel. This she held fast to against the flood of negative impressions coming from her mother.

It was not a large pension, five rooms, and at best it provided a modest living for her and her mother. Nor, to belie its name, was it luxurious or unique in any way. Four of the rooms offered pleasant views out the back overlooking a footbridge that crossed the narrow, white-water-filled river pocked with boulders. The furnishings were tasteful, but the one really fine piece, an armoire with mahogany veneer and ormolu mounts, they kept in the hallway on the second floor as a storage space for linen. The breakfast room on the ground floor was, like their own apartment, small, dark and dreary. Guests, Frieda noticed, tended not to linger there, however bright the centerpiece or fragrant the warm bread.

In some ways the pension seemed to Frieda an extension of herself, as if her skin were stretched to enclose a personal prison. She had scrubbed and buffed every inch of it a thousand times. Often when falling asleep, some obscure detail—the pattern of cracks in the tile of the foyer floor, or the chips in the base of the lyre-bottom table—would burst suddenly and vividly into her mind. In other ways the guestrooms held an exotic fascination; they were like close friends who lived second lives, separate and unknown to her. Once when she was eleven she had sneaked out of the apartment in the middle of the night and had made her way to one of the vacant rooms. Stealthily she had opened the door. Light from the moon spilled across a corner of the carefully made-up bed. Lying in that bed, her face at the edge of the moonlight, Frieda had felt herself a princess. "Are you crazy?" her mother had shouted the next morning as she dragged Frieda back to the apartment. "That is a guestroom!"

In 1962, a few weeks after her twentieth birthday, Frieda had left the pension and taken a bus to Salzburg. There she rented a small upstairs room and found work in a coffee house. It had been a daring—even now it seemed so—perhaps desperate move. At first her mother raged by post and telephone. Then after a few weeks there came no further word. Frieda's letters were unanswered; when she telephoned the pension Erna would hang up without speaking. Finally, a letter arrived from the family's doctor. Erna was scheduled for an operation; her left breast had to be removed. At the funeral Frieda counted back. Following that operation, Erna had managed to hold onto life, and to her, for an additional twenty years plus one month and two weeks.

§

At the time of Erna's death, two of the rooms were being let fulltime. One guest, Herr Reutter, dispensed stamps at the local post office. He was a pleasant balding man in his late fifties who read French romantic poets, was given to occasional drunks and smoked incessantly; at night his dry hacking cough seeped through the walls. He had many friends and was often away in the evenings. His gossip was probably the most accurate and certainly the most entertaining in the village. Occasionally he and Frieda played chess.

The winter before Erna's death, Herr Reutter met a woman in the next village and had given up alcohol. Frieda's mother, even as she lay dying, had worried that he would soon leave and move in with the woman. Before that she worried that he would die from the smoking; either way there would be a vacancy. Frieda felt both shame and disdain when Erna reduced Herr Reutter to a steady source of shillings, but she said nothing. A decision had long been made to not dispute Erna's picture of reality; its walls, unlike the walls of the Pension Alhambra, were impenetrable.

The other boarder, Herr Robinig, seemed to Frieda a darker presence, though the darkness lay behind a solicitous façade. Herr Robinig regularly brought the dying Erna flowers and sweets; he leaned over her wasting body and called her his spring chicken. A tall man, five years older than Frieda, with fine graceful hands, he had been transferred to the village by a national company to manage its woolens shop. Frieda would see him sliding past the tables and racks, his long fingers smoothing the sweaters and scarves. Erna used to say, "If only your father had been like Herr Robinig, a gentleman and a practical man."

One night, perhaps a month after Herr Robinig moved in and a year before Erna died, Frieda went to pick up the dishes from his evening meal. He was seated at a small table reading a catalog. As she reached for the tray, Herr Robinig turned and studied her over his glasses.

"You are looking particularly attractive tonight, Frieda," he said, placing the long fingers of his right hand on her forearm.

Frieda stood very still for a moment, holding her breath until his fingers released themselves. "I think not, Herr Robinig."

"But it is so," Herr Robinig insisted. "In a place this small people forget to look. They no longer see you. Your very familiarity makes you invisible. You no longer see even yourself."

"My mother is waiting, Herr Robinig."

"Ah, of course." Herr Robinig laughed softly, recognizing as she did the significance of those words coming from a woman nearly forty. "You know, Frieda, when I was a child our family had an orchard. My favorite fruit was always the pear. Today, I cannot eat them. They are hard and tasteless or soft and messy. I am surprised I ever liked them."

"I'm sorry, Herr Robinig, but you are being too allegorical for me. Or are you saying you do not wish to be served pears? That I can remember."

Herr Robinig smiled. "It is I who am sorry. I'm not good at this kind of thing. I was simply trying to offer you a drink. I am a single man, a lonely man, every day farther from my youth." He raised small glass of clear liquid and held it to the light. "Pear schnapps, Frieda. The essence of the pear without the chewing or the mess. The adult way to enjoy a pear. But I understand, if your mother is waiting."

In the end he made a clumsy pass that she physically resisted and which left her angry and trembling in the hallway. Of this she said nothing to her mother. It was a good decision, she realized a few days later when she conveyed to Erna the village whispers that Herr Robinig was a harsh employer. Erna would accept none of it. All such talk, she said, sprang from jealousy. A man like that, a man with such refined qualities, would not long remain their boarder. A rich woman would snare him or the company would promote him to Innsbruck or Vienna (forgetting, Frieda thought, that he had come from Innsbruck, a likely demotion). In either event, there would be a vacancy.

§

From her mother's death arose many small responsibilities. With the sexton she prepared the black-bordered death announcement that he laminated and tacked onto the noticeboard before the church. There were details of the funeral and burial; long letters to and from relatives; the intricacies of the estate, principally the process of transferring the Pension Alhambra into her name. Meanwhile, the snow season had ended and the spring schedule was crowded. Bookings made months before arrived or cancelled, long-time customers called on short notice and had to be worked in. And through it all was the laundry, the cooking and the endless cleaning. Still appearing in her mind now and then was an image from her childhood: her mother, seeming huge, hands-on-hips, a rag over one shoulder, demanding that she do it again, that she keep doing it until she had done it right.

She was free now, she told herself. She could hike one of the trails, lunch with a friend, or let it all go and take the bus into Salzburg for a day. But the rhythm of the work, the physical exertion, the ritual of cleaning provided a curious comfort. She found herself, when her tasks were finished, looking for some little project— polish the door handles?—to extend it further.

In June the Hardings came from America for a week's stay. Frieda was hosing off the sidewalk when they arrived; she greeted them in the parking area before the garage. Dr. Harding was a thin pale man with a trim nearly white beard, a professor, Frieda soon learned, of dentistry. Mrs. Harding's dark hair had its first traces of gray, her eyes were intently blue. She was wearing a lovely pale blue scarf over her shoulders and a variety of perfume that Frieda found tantalizing and elusive. Enthusiastic, her German nearly fluent, Marta Harding poured out her origins.

"I was born near Chemnitz, now Karl-Marx-Stadt in the east," she explained. "My father had been killed and my mother carried me west before the borders were secured. She eventually married an American soldier. I grew up in Massachusetts."

Marta had kept up her German and taught a course each semester at the same university where her husband taught. But her principal career was in real estate, developing properties, buying and selling them. She seemed to Frieda a piece of herself who had escaped.

The next afternoon Frieda was outside pinching aged blossoms from her geraniums when the Hardings returned from a hike. Marta Harding dropped to the ground near where Frieda was working.

"This place is paradise," she exclaimed, stretching out her legs.

Frieda asked where they had gone for their picnic.

"Well, we took the lift up onto the alm and hiked until we found ourselves in a lovely meadow. It was beautiful and we were all alone, can you believe it? It had a southwestern exposure with two snow-capped peaks in clear view and hints of others. Magical! Several hectares of open land. We could even hear cowbells coming from just over the rise. And you will never guess what I did."

Frieda shook her head.

"I sat there and I imagined all the building sites I could sell in that meadow. I planned out the roads. I divided up the parcels so every house had an excellent view and a sense of privacy." Marta giggled. "I would never actually do such a thing of course. And I couldn't, even if I wanted to. It's just a habit. But my man teased me. He said, Marta, if you had your way, this would become a place that you, yourself, would never want to come back to! Isn't that funny?"

Listening to Marta Harding laugh reminded Frieda of one of the few times she had ever agreed with Herr Robinig. Commenting on Herr Reutter, he had said: "A happy person always amazes me. I ask myself, 'How can it be?'"

§

One evening during the week of the Hardings' visit, Herr Robinig came to Frieda's apartment with a box of chocolates. He glanced at the egg in her hand and then at the table cluttered with jars of paint, birdseed and colored beads.

"Your decorated eggs are the talk of the village, Frieda."

"Thank you, Herr Robinig, but I doubt that is so."

"I assure you it is. But you believe nothing I say." He bowed slightly, offering the candies.

Feeling obligated, Frieda invited him in for tea. Herr Robinig took a seat and when the tea was ready, he rested the cup and saucer on his crossing knee, tugging gently at the crease of his slacks.

"Your business is going well by all appearances," he told her. "The rooms are full every night, and the establishment is well kept. The meals have improved, for my part. Your mother would be pleased."

"Thank you, Herr Robinig, though I doubt she would be pleased. To her the meals were just another expense and I am spending more on them. Incidentally, I have decided to sell the pension. You should know."

This sudden declaration, surprising even to Frieda, brought genuine shock to the face of Herr Robinig. "Is it because Herr Reutter has decided to marry? You'll find another boarder. The Alhambra has a strong reputation."

"It has nothing to do with Herr Reutter. I was born in this pension and I don't intend to die here."

"I see," Herr Robinig said quietly. "Excuse me. It is your business, of course." He lifted one of her empty egg shells and held it briefly in his open palm as if weighing it.

§

On Sunday the Hardings took Frieda out to dinner. They all had the house specialty, *Forella im sekt*, and each chose their trout from a glass tank near the door. As they were walking back to the pension, Frieda mentioned that she was considering selling.

"Well, you must not," Marta Harding said at once. Shattered by the abrupt statement, Frieda walked on a few steps while Marta translated this news for Dr.

Harding. "How long has the pension been in your family?" Marta asked when they caught up.

"My father bought it before the war, but he left to become a pilot."

Dr. Harding said something in English that Frieda could not understand. Then, Marta asked and Frieda nodded. Yes, he did not return. His is one of the many names inscribed on the monument that you saw near the church.

"But he got away from here," Frieda continued. "I've hardly been beyond Salzburg. He flew. I have never flown. I have never seen an ocean. Am I bound by a decision he made and then abandoned?"

As Marta translated Frieda's words for her husband, the three of them continued along the narrow walkway as a continuous stream of cars rushed past them on the cobbled street.

"You would leave the village?" Marta asked.

"Yes, I think so."

When they had crossed the bridge and started up toward the pension, Frieda caught a whiff of Marta's fine perfume.

"It would be a mistake," Marta said firmly. "This is paradise. This is your security. And you have all that history to think about."

§

Near the end of the Harding's stay, Frieda invited them down to her apartment. It was a tradition Erna had started years before. She had been quite idiosyncratic about whom she invited. Some guests returned for years and never received an invitation. Others were chosen before the end of their first visit. Erna would seat them around the kitchen table, the only table in the apartment and serve them mint tea and cake.

As a child Frieda had dreaded these encounters, which for her were compulsory. She was ashamed of their small, squalid apartment, the chipped china, her mother's raspy voice. For Erna, however, all aspects of the encounters were significant. With medical doctors she would inquire about her own symptoms and those of her friends; with others she discussed music, literature, politics. If someone mentioned travel Erna squeezed them dry of detail. To stimulate conversation with one guest, she would spend the proceeds gained from one she had had with another. Even the humbleness of their quarters served, in Erna's mind, to increase the frequency and size of the guests' parting tips.

"I have never felt so good in my life," Marta Harding announced as she accepted the tea. "The beauty, the walking, this air, the complete lack of responsibility. Herr Harding sends his regrets by the way. He's tired, and the continual German gives him a headache."

Frieda offered to get something for Dr. Harding's head.

"You are so sweet, Frieda," Marta Harding said, laughing. "I swear you are just like this pension, this village: beautiful, simple, pure."

"I am not," Frieda retorted angrily, thus violating one of Erna's cardinal rules that you never under any circumstances argue with a guest. "I am not beautiful. I am not simple, and I am damn tired of being pure."

Marta Harding looked shocked for a moment. Then she laughed and threw her arms around Frieda.

"I'm sorry. I am being so selfish. It's just that I want you to be here when we come back. I want this place to always be just as it is now. At home everything changes. We come to Europe in search of things that don't change. Of course, that's silly and selfish. You must do whatever your heart tells you."

Frieda and Marta cried the morning the Hardings left. Frieda gave Marta ten of her decorated eggs and Marta invited her to visit them in the States.

Later, when she entered the Hardings' room to clean, Frieda closed and locked the door. It was a sunny morning and the room was warm and light. She sat down on the edge of the bed and looked around. They had argued here, made love, talked about her. She drew back the fetter bet and slid beneath it. It was not difficult to find the side Marta had slept on: that wonderful perfume permeated the pillowcase. Frieda placed her hands beneath the pillow, curled up and closed her eyes.

A half hour later she woke with a jerk; she felt hot and clammy. Though her face was still pressed against the pillow, she could no longer smell the perfume. But the voice from her dream still boomed in her ears:

"Here you are lying on someone else's soiled sheets while the pension is half cleaned and guests are expected and the mid-day sun shines like shame through the window!"

The voice, Frieda realized, was not her mother's voice but her own. Nothing remained of her mother. Nothing.

She sat up and looked out the window. Just upstream from the footbridge, torrents of water tumbled and frothed as it pushed past a large boulder. All her life she had heard that rushing water and watched as it threw itself against the boulder. The boulder had been there long before she was born, before the bridge was constructed, before the pension was named, or built or even imagined. And still the water came, frothing and tumbling on its long journey from icy peaks to the sea.

Frieda rose and turned. She stripped the bed and pushed the used linens into a pillowcase that she placed in the hallway outside the door. From the mahogany armoire with its ormolu mounts she removed a set of ironed, fresh-smelling bedding. When the bed had been remade and the room cleaned and straightened, Frieda paused at the doorway. The room was no longer the room where the Hardings had made love and talked about her. That room was gone, as her mother was gone. The room was now a guestroom. That's what Frieda told herself.

THE WALRUS VISITS

On the plane that morning flying from San Francisco to Chicago, Albert Morgan was assigned a middle seat in the middle section, coach. It was early June and a full house. Kids and parents crowded in among the usual business crowd. Morgan boarded late and his cumbersome passage from aisle to seat created a small turmoil along the row. He was a large man, thick in the hips, and he lowered himself carefully into the last remaining empty seat.

"Stuck in the middle," he said aloud, "quite literally."

The businesswoman on his right chuckled. The teenager on his left remained frozen beneath his Rockies cap.

"They should have issued me a shoehorn," Morgan added into the ear of the young man.

"What?"

"A shoehorn. You know what a shoehorn is?"

"Not really." The young man looked terrified.

"You're not a musician, I take it. I play violin myself. Very well, actually."

"Cool."

"That's right. Have you had any musical training?"

"Not really."

"Not really." Morgan sighed and bent forward with a grunt to squeeze his duffel bag under the seat in front of him. "Well, consider the shoehorn if you ever do. A good horn player is always in demand."

When Morgan straightened up he noted that the boy had buried his face in the in-flight magazine. Morgan leaned his head against the back of the seat and closed his eyes. You're the one who's terrified, he thought.

§

In one of O'Hare's high-ceilinged and crowded corridors, Albert Morgan stopped with his luggage and stood for a moment. He did this for no reason other than to collect himself, something he felt it necessary to do frequently. And to breathe, and to ponder the world swirling around him. It felt as if he and his luggage had taken the form of an oddly shaped boulder that had tumbled from an eroding cliff eons before only to find itself set down in a torrent of perpetually cascading water. Water that would over time slowly and surely grind him away. No, he thought, correcting himself, not "would"—had been, and presently was, grinding him away. He could feel that at his core, though if the matter were evaluated solely on the evidence of his bathroom scale he was actually getting larger.

Morgan telephoned his daughter but Linda, his ex-wife, answered.

"One of life's little constants, Al Morgan arriving at the very last minute."

"So, how's married life, Linda? Get it right this time."

"It's nice, Al. You should try it sometime."

"I did."

"Sort of you did. Anyway, it starts in just two hours." She sounded frazzled. "We're having a little thing over here afterwards. Erica and her friends. You're invited, of course."

"Is Erica…"

"She's dressing. It's a big deal, Al, you should know that. We'll have to meet you at the auditorium." She gave directions. "You can sit with Nick and me."

It had started to rain. Morgan, whose only car was twenty years old, fumbled among the knobs and switches of the rental before he located the wipers. He had to park three blocks from the auditorium. In the crowded foyer people were shaking down their umbrellas and smelling of damp fabric. The inside of Morgan's shirt felt moist and sticky. He stomped his feet and went into the men's room. He took off his suitcoat and had to bend nearly double to get his head in front of the electric hand dryer.

"They call this progress," he said out the side of his mouth to a man washing his hands. "I remember when schools had cloth towels on a roller. I grew up in schools. My mother worked in the office, my father was the music teacher. Those cloth towels on a roller. Remember those?"

"You're lucky you got hair," the man said, turning to leave. "Some of us ain't so lucky."

When Morgan came out of the restroom the foyer was nearly empty. Linda was nowhere to be seen and he would not have recognized her husband had they bumped into each other.

The pianist struck the opening bars of the processional and Morgan rushed to find a seat. (She had chosen, he noted with harried satisfaction, one of Elgar's less familiar "Pomp and Circumstance" marches.) The audience rose and turned toward the back of the auditorium. Two columns of students, blue-robed beneath tilting mortarboards entered and passed quickly down the aisles. Though he tried to scan each face, Morgan did not recognize his daughter.

He remembered something then, an incident that had occurred nine years before, a few months after he had moved west. Erica, age five and traveling alone, was flying out to visit him for the first time. He arrived late at the airport and had to race down the long concourse to her arrival gate. There he found the desk vacant, the waiting area nearly empty. Out of breath and close to panic, he noticed a little girl playing a few yards away. Her hair was the same color as Erica's and she was about the size his daughter should be after a half year of growth. The child glanced up at him. Her eyes were as large and as hazel as Erica's but her nose seemed broader, her mouth wider. No, he decided, she was definitely not Erica; he would know his own daughter. The little girl was staring at him. Morgan squinted. Surely, he thought, they would not just leave her unattended. "Erica?" Hearing him, the child had turned and run away, and Morgan, taking a closer look at the monitor, discovered that his daughter's flight had been delayed forty-five minutes.

The valedictorian was beginning her speech. "You're lucky you got hair," Morgan muttered in her direction. "Some of us ain't so lucky."

§

Erica lived with Linda and Nick in a large old brick house on a quiet street in a suburb west of the city. The ceilings on the first floor were nine feet high, and Morgan stood in the summer kitchen admiring the distant light fixture. Nick passed through carrying a CD player with its speakers and extension cords balanced on top. He was younger than Morgan, younger than Linda. Said to be an avid golfer, his black hair carefully parted. Something to do with banking, Morgan remembered.

"The wiring is old," Nick said. "That's one of the problems."

"These go out?" Morgan asked, pointing toward a stack of soda cans.

"There's a tub of ice out back," Nick said.

The rain had stopped and the yard smelled washed and alive. Ten six-packs, each in its milky plastic wrapper. Linda and another woman were arranging trays of food on a long table. The door opened and Erica descended the stairs carrying a box of candles.

"Twenty, Dad," she answered. "And they all want to meet you."

The button pinned to the collar of her blouse was red. In its center was a yellow question mark.

They ate in warm twilight, the graduates in the center of the lawn, the adults at the picnic table near the door.

"Think I'll take a few shots," Nick said, picking up his camera. "I got one of her coming down the aisle. If it turns out we'll send you a copy." He left for the table of graduates, shooting as he approached.

"It's the absent father syndrome," Linda said. "It's not fair. She puts you on a pedestal."

"Better be a big one."

"Nick's her father in everything but name. When she's late for class he drives her. When she broke her ankle that time in soccer he carried her up and down the stairs." Linda straightened her back and placed her forearms on the table. "Deep down she hates you for leaving."

Morgan ran a finger along his sweating beer bottle and looked over at the graduates.

"I'm still with the symphony, of course. And there's a quartet, some solo work, as Erica has probably mentioned. The usual array of students. That's what I'm doing. Thank you for not asking."

"And the composing? I read where Philip performed the sonata last winter."

"Yes, he sent a tape." Morgan scraped the few remaining grains of rice to the edge of his plate. He had composed his sonata shortly after Erica was born. It was said to be generous, warm. Of his published pieces the most accessible to the audience. That had been a long time ago.

"The sonata was well received, that's what I read."

"Yes," Morgan said wearily. "It always has been."

Nick returned to the table and set down the camera. "Mark and I are going to hang the piñata,"He said. "Back in a minute."

Let me help," Morgan offered, starting to rise.

"No need, we got it."

Morgan sat back down. He said to Linda, "When I was admiring the high ceilings of your lovely home your husband thought I was inspecting the wiring."

"There are things he'd rather be doing than hanging your kid's damn piñata."

"Christ, Linda."

She sighed. "Your coming has all of us a little wacky."

§

Albert Morgan was beginning to enjoy the rental car. Compared to the relic back home it felt snug and peppy. On Route 294 the next afternoon heading south he nimbly switched from lane to lane while tapping a fingernail against the steering wheel. The tapping was his attempt to adjust his sensibilities to the music pouring from the radio. Moments after entering the car Erica had configured the buttons to tune in her three favorite rock stations and her fingers danced nimbly from one to the other hopping over the commercials.

"Now, that's an old one," she said. "I mean really old. Jefferson Starship. That might even be Airplane."

She pushed a button, head spinning around. "Wow, another Stingray! You know, I've never seen a dirty Stingray. I never see any Stingrays around home, come to think of it."

"They steal them!" Morgan exclaimed, suddenly feeling wildly inspired. "Two out of three before they're a year old. This guy I knew in college. He was on the periphery of a ring of car thieves. You never knew what he might be driving from week to week. Two out of three, that's what he told me about Corvettes one time. The percentage might be different now. That was years ago, of course. Before Starship probably, maybe even Airplane."

They were driving downstate to Randall, the small town where he had spent his childhood and where, as his father used to claim, he had been only the violin student within fifty miles. Fifty miles being the distance they had to drive for lessons after the old man decided young Al had talent and needed an outside teacher. Not just an outside teacher, a youth orchestra and other young people "who are like you." Meaning unlike the riffraff, into whose skulls the elder Morgan was obligated, day after day, year after year, to instill some sense of musical appreciation.

The landscape eased from suburban to rural. Erica's favorite stations faded to two and then to one. At one point not far from Randall they spotted four Corvettes parked on different farmyard lawns, a yellow one, then a red, a black and finally a silver one all within three miles of one another.

"Well," his daughter announced, "now we know where they fence them."

Morgan roared, feeling delirious behind his sunglasses. It was going to be all right. It was going to work out. That morning at the tri-lateral negotiations which settled who would go where with whom and for how long, Linda had scoffed at the idea of Randall. "You're in Chicago, Al. You got museums, restaurants, concert halls, sporting events, the Lake, parks galore. And you're taking your daughter to Randall? I don't get it. Has this got something to do with your father?" For her part, Erica had shrugged and said, "Whatever."

§

The motel they chose had a large pool and shared an intersection with three fast-food franchises. They swam: "The walrus at play," Morgan had announced floating on his back—and then they crossed the street to dinner.

Seated in a plastic chair, his arms on a plastic table along with the wrappers and boxes and those pathetic little wrinkled containers half full of ketchup, Morgan observed his daughter staring vaguely at the other customers seated in seeming isolation from one another. She's bored to distraction, he thought. She doesn't want to be here. We have tonight, tomorrow and much of Sunday together. I don't know what we're going to do and she doesn't know how she's going to stand it.

"The indigenous cuisine," he said, breaking the silence and recognizing the banality of his proclamation even as he proclaimed it, "the industrial hamburger, the never-was-an-actual-potato kind of fry, the maybe non-dairy milkshake. Tomorrow we'll try an uptown, waitressed, hoity-toity kind of place. See if we can rustle up some real grub."

Erica did not indicate that she even heard him. But a moment later she asked a question: "Is everyone old in this place? Even the people working here are old, can you believe it? I mean what's with that? Back home it's kids work in places like this."

It was true. Large, lump-like people sat with their trays of food in clusters and in isolation. Behind the counter, dyed-hair beneath cute little caps, scrawny tendon-streaked necks held up crinkled smiles. We have ideals, he thought as he looked about: the pretty face, the squared jaw, the straight nose, the breadth of shoulder, the trim waist, the swelling breast, the bulging bicep, the sculpted six pack (especially good for modeling underwear), and then we have people.

These were people. He was people. The only violinist within fifty miles, and one of the people.

"I left when I was seventeen," he said, as if that offered some explanation. "Off to Philadelphia."

"The scholarship."

"Yes," Morgan said. "The greatest moment in your grandfather's life."

"His...?" Erica was looking at him strangely.

Morgan rousted himself, "So, it's back on the tour bus and off for the evening's entertainment."

§

Morgan conducted a tour of the town with desperate enthusiasm. The house where he had grown up, the bungalow his parents purchased after they retired and before they moved to Arizona where his father had promptly died following an argument with a man over a croquet game.

An argument over a croquet game; Morgan could not get that oddity out of his mind. The exploding of his father's heart may have had nothing to do with the argument or the croquet game but Morgan was incapable of divorcing the loss from how it happened. "He was still fuming," Morgan's mother had explained. Die and you become a story. That's the way the world works, the way we get on. How could he explain this truth to the muse sitting stoically in the passenger seat?

"There was a violinist," he began, "a man named Huberman, Bronislaw Huberman. This man accomplished many things but what I remember most about him is that he managed to have his Strad stolen not once but twice. After he died that's what everyone remembered about him, that he could not hold onto his violin."

"Like the Corvettes," Erica said, her fingers slowly turning the knob in search of more music. By some process Morgan had missed, the hand he now studied had lost its dimpled chubbiness and had assumed a graceful line and soft luster that one day all manner of creams and gentle soaps might try and fail to replicate.

"Yes, but my point…"

"We should check the pawn shops around here. If this is where they dump the 'vettes maybe this guy's violin is gathering dust on some shelf in Randall."

"You could think of it as a graduation," Morgan added topically, but fruitlessly. "You die and you become a story. It's like a promotion."

"Think how many Corvettes you could buy if you found a Strad in a pawn shop. Of course the guy in the shop wouldn't know its true value. You pick it up for say a hundred bucks. Sell it at an auction in New York for a mil or more. Fat city. Want to take another swim before they close the pool?"

"There's a place I want to show you first."

He drove around the corner and down several blocks before stopping in front of a large square building that appeared to have been abandoned years before. Old dark brick. Three floors of small windows awaiting the wrecking ball.

"K through eight," Morgan explained. "We didn't have a junior high."

"Where you went to school?"

"Yes, and where your grandmother managed the office. Ran the whole place really, the principal was a dunce. And your grandfather taught the world to sing in this building. Not just students. The whole town was singing. Three school choirs, the Randall Town Choir. For a while a choir that only senior citizens could join. Everybody sang. Even if you couldn't sing, you were encouraged to join. There were gradations, you see. Some choirs you auditioned for. You came and stood in front of him and you sang solo. You sang melody, you sang harmony, he determined your qualifications and your range. For others you just showed up and bellowed, which, by the way, is how your grandmother described it. Every holiday and public event he herded them onto the stage, one choir after another culminating in a grand finale where everyone was jammed up there together, a sea of white tops and dark bottoms that he led through his famous medley of patriotic songs."

Morgan and his daughter exited the car. They approached the front doors and peered through the windows, their hands cupped around their eyes.

"Her office was up those stairs. On the right."

"Cool," his daughter said.

He marched to the back of the building, she following a few feet behind. He felt himself on the hunt.

"The band room," he said, squatting down, knees popping, to look through the half window into a dark and empty space. "'The Cave' as he called it. The cafeteria was next door and the place always smelled of fish sticks or what they called barbecued beef, a substance that wasn't barbecued but probably contained beef. Risers in back for choir practice. Metal chairs arced around the podium for band rehearsals. They said he threw those chairs across the room when he was frustrated. I never saw that myself, though his temper was legendary and you crossed him at your peril.

"A piano, of course. He could play quite well, and he knew enough about each instrument to give a student a start. A phonograph that looked like a fat suitcase always on the desk. For the younger kids he played *The Grand Canyon Suite*. 'On the Trail,' of course. Dad in front marching around like a mule. Then came the *Peer Gynt Suites.* 'Morning Mood.' Tears would form in his eyes as he stood up there watching it touch them. 'In the Hall of the Mountain King.' 'Listen to this!' he would shout, and begin talking about trolls." Morgan leaned back on his heels, closed his eyes and sighed. In this cave his father had been king of the mountain: tempestuous, demanding, caring, a master of his craft.

When he looked up he realized that Erica had drifted away to the street behind the school. She was walking back now. He had been talking to himself. For how long, he had no idea.

"God, that is gross back there. Bird poop everywhere."

He noticed the smell now. So familiar.

"Starlings," he said, grunting his way back to his feet. "Starlings on every limb lined up like Muscovites. When I was a boy men used to gather with shotguns and fire birdshot blindly up into those trees. A flurry of explosions, then squawks, screams, the rush of wings, the sharp smell of gunpowder. Birds tumbling down through the branches."

It seemed amazing to him now that such a thing could have happened. But he remembered it clearly. The fathers coming out of their houses at dusk, weapons in hand, bright shells in lines along their vests. Like the mustering of an ad hoc militia. Guns blazing in the middle of town. It really was amazing. And should it not amaze his daughter that such a thing had happened?

"Dad, could we go back to the pool now and have a swim before it gets too late?"

"It won't get too late," Morgan responded, his voice harsh. "I determine what's late and what isn't. I'm still your dad, remember?"

Erica looked suddenly smaller to him, slumped, thin. She turned away, grabbing the railing of an old fire escape.

"I just meant they close the pool at nine. There's a sign," she added quietly. "That's all."

Morgan felt it right through him. "Of course. I'm sorry. Let's do go back."

"No, it's okay. I was rude. This really is interesting."

Meaning, Morgan assumed, that she wished it were, that it should be, that there was something wrong with her that it wasn't.

He took her arm and they started back toward the car. The thick starling smell seemed to force its way into his lungs. It caused him to breathe in short quick gasps the way the birds had, their wings splayed, breasts up, dying on the pavement.

§

The button the next morning was pink. In black letters it said: "I'm braless."

They packed towels, swimsuits, sandwiches, bottles of juice. They drove down a gravel road to where it intersected a railroad track.

"How far is it?" Erica asked when they got out.

The tracks stretched ahead of them on a high bed that fell away to the right into fields and to the left into patches of trees bordering a stream. The warming sun had begun to release creosote vapors from the old ties.

"We'll have to cross a long trestle, I remember that. I think the trestle is beyond that curve." Seeing her expression, he added, "It's not as far as it looks."

Hiking was a thing they did together. Morgan sought her out by removing her from the viscous milieu of her age and station and exposing her to earth and air. It took them forty-five minutes to reach the curve, a curve that swept so gently they had to look back to realize they were on it, and then another twenty to the trestle.

Guided by his questions, she brought him up to date: the musical she had been in, the classes she would take in the fall, the camp she'd attend in July. They could talk well enough and parts of each of them reached toward a vaguely remembered union. But there remained a certain distance. Morgan saw it as a line she wouldn't cross; a line in her psyche etched precisely where his leaving had cut her.

Beyond the trestle, a path descended into thickly-vined and buzzing underbrush. Morgan sensed a foreboding.

"Do you recognize poison ivy?" he asked. "It's different from the poison oak I've showed you in California."

"Dad, I live in Illinois, remember?"

He remembered.

The pond was still there, though disappointingly small and not as pristine as in his memory. The tilted frame of a tepee had been erected nearby; the remains of a campfire contained beer cans and a plastic, half-melted potato chip bag. But they were alone, the water cool, and where the sun struck it, a soft green. Water bugs stalked the surface. In the fall, he remembered, migrating waterfowl would pause here and work the fields of newly harvested corn.

Erica swam well. She dove to the bottom and brought up rocks, a belt buckle, a crawdad with its pincers searching the air. Later, they lay in the shallow water, their backs on the sand; the slightest movement of their submerged legs caused the fine warm silt to rise and resettle.

Erica stroked his beard with the tips of her fingers. "It's so smooth when it's wet."

"I've had it a long time," he said sleepily. "I started growing it the year you were born."

"Think you'll ever cut if off?" she asked, as above them a blue jay scolded their intrusion.

"I consider it now and then."

Erica sat up suddenly and cupped his face in her hands. "Dad, promise you won't do it unless I'm there. Promise?"

Morgan promised. He also confessed that he had not recognized her in the processional. Then he told her about the experience he had years before at the airport.

"Then that's how I'll recognize you," she announced triumphantly. "You'll be the one looking for me."

More than the words, her ruddy stamina and hardy good humor cheered him. Still, on the long walk back with the afternoon heat rising from the rails, it occurred to him that their strongest bond might be a shared fear of non-recognition.

§

On Sunday they ran the film in reverse. The stations returned, dim then stronger. The lanes multiplied from two to four to eight. Even the button with its large yellow question mark reappeared against her collarbone.

Nearing the city and immersed again in the jarring sounds pouring from the radio, Erica happily resumed her complex suburban intensity. As she assembled the change for the first toll booth, she confided that she had missed a party on Friday.

"Same old gang," she said. "A day at Great America."

Morgan apologized as he took the handful of coins and tossed them into the basket.

"That's okay, Dad. Tonight's another. Endless parties, that's your daughter."

"I was thinking of dinner," he said. "Maybe a movie." Then, seeing her disappointment, he added, "But I'm bushed. Let's save it for when you come out."

Released, Erica punched a button and the resulting sound sent Morgan swinging the rental car out into the fast lane.

SNAKE

Western diamondback rattler, the sign said. *Crotalus atrox.* A good-sized snake, thick, four-feet long or better, confined and enraged behind a wall of thick glass. The boy liked to stand nearby watching as people passed: how it struck at them, smashing its mouth and fangs against the glass, smearing the surface with a milky, semen-like substance, the sound of it hitting. He was thrilled by the speed and violence of it, by the sudden slap against the glass, by the slight nausea he felt at this cruelty masquerading as science, by his own guilty pleasure.

NAIL RUN

Jack ducked his head and entered the old trailer. When he had closed the door he straightened up and paused for a moment to enjoy the relative quiet. He could still hear the wind buffeting against the metal walls, but now it was outside and away and it could no longer touch him.

On the counter the alarm clock was ticking. 3:48. He had hoped it would be later. He pulled loose the top two snaps on his leather jacket and walked back to the bedroom. Susan was lying on the bed with the baby. She had been dozing. A roach was smashed in the ashtray and he could smell the lingering remains of the marijuana.

"Need some nails," he said.

Susan nodded and he stepped over to the dresser and took his red helmet and cupped it in his arm like a football.

"Get something for dinner," she said.

"Like what?"

She thought for a moment. The baby was waking and she stroked the soft hairs on his head.

"Get some tortillas. We can make tacos. I got salsa, beans and cheese, and I'll pick some greens. We'll do a salad."

He fingered in his wallet, separating the bills from the food stamps. "Some beer?"

"Sure." The baby began to cry. Susan sat up against the headboard and put the child to her breast.

"Goddamned wind."

She nodded, looking out the window at the waving branches.

§

On the motorcycle, riding along the twisting dirt road, Jack felt the wind slam against him whenever he came out on the exposed side of the ridge. But later, on the valley floor, he felt it less. Here the road was paved and relatively level and the broad curves mimicked the course of the river. He pushed the bike up to fifty miles an hour and leaned down and against the centrifugal force. Now he was making the wind and creating the noise, and inside the helmet he found a stillness. It was like the stillness he noticed when he had been running the chainsaw for a long time and the roar of the motor seemed to fade into the background. That was the best thing about motorcycles and chainsaws: the quiet you could find hidden within the noise.

Twenty minutes later he parked the motorcycle near the south wall of the store, balanced the helmet on the odometer and handlebars and walked inside. He selected a package of tortillas and two bags of peanuts. From the cooler and took out a sixteen ounce can of beer and walked to the checker. He paid cash for the beer and gave food stamps for the tortillas and the nuts.

Outside, he carefully set the can on the gas tank and balanced the bags of nuts on the seat. Then he crouched down and dropped the tortillas into the nearest of the scarred leather saddle bags. He had parked in the sun on the lee side of the store and when he stood, he pulled loose the snaps on his jacket, one by one from the top to the bottom. He tore open a bag of nuts with his teeth, puffed it out with his hands and set it back down against the other bag without taking any. Then he opened the beer and took a long drink.

From a shirt pocket he took out a pouch of tobacco and some papers and carefully rolled a cigarette. He smoked slowly, alternating drags off the cigarette with swallows of beer, and as he smoked he looked out across the road toward the forest-covered hills and now and then he scratched his beard with the edge of his thumb.

He was finishing the cigarette when a battered, dust-covered pickup pulled into the lot and stopped a few feet away. The driver stuck his head out the open window and grinned at Jack.

"Thought you were busy building a room on for the baby."

Jack nodded slowly. "Goddamned wind."

The driver lifted a beer can from between his legs and took a swig. He had long stringy hair that was receding from his tan forehead. His nose was large and beaked and his pale blue eyes held a look that Jack had seen in the eyes of many of his male friends. He saw it in his own eyes sometimes.

"I woke at four this morning and it was blowing already," the driver said. "I knew there was no sense going out. It must'a blown all night."

"It's been blowing day and night for three days," Jack said. "It gets inside and drives me crazy." He picked up the open bag of nuts, poured out a palm full and tossed them into his mouth. He took a swallow of beer and asked, "Catching any salmon?"

"The last week in May was great. Caught over seven hundred dollars' worth three days running. Then it fell off and now with this wind there's no fishing. You'd need a large boat to go out in this."

Jack made a motion with the nuts, the driver nodded and Jack tossed him the unopened package. A moment later a bright green, late model car entered the lot and parked a few feet away. Jack looked at the car but didn't recognize the make. As a kid he had known all the makes and models. It was something he had been proud of: how he could glance at a car and tell you the year it was made, the company that made it and the model. But that boy had been an early casualty, and now the newer cars all looked more or less the same to him.

The man who got out of the car was dressed for jogging with white shorts and clean white running shoes; on his jersey was the insignia of the local junior college. His legs were stocky and brown and his graying hair was combed in neat waves.

"Jack," the man said with a solemn nod as he passed, and then nodding to the man in the pickup: "Tom."

Jack and Tom nodded, and when the man had entered the store they looked at each other for a moment without speaking. Jack emptied his beer and smashed the can with his boot. He picked it up and tossed it into a box against the wall that had "Aluminum" written on the front.

"One of these?" Tom asked, waving the remains of his six-pack.

Jack nodded and caught the can Tom tossed him. He set it on the gas tank, poured the remaining nuts into his mouth and rolled another cigarette.

"Listen," he said. "Even down here in this cranny you can hear it in the trees. Do you hear it?"

"Yeah, I hear it." Tom looked at the hills. "It's blowing like hell up there, I can see it. It won't stop before dark."

Jack lit the cigarette. He tapped the top of the beer can with his finger and opened it.

"I plan on having the frame up by the end of the week," he said. "I would have finished the deck today if I had stuck with it."

"What are your dimensions?"

"Eight by ten. Nothing fancy. I bought the flooring and the structural members but I milled the siding out of a fir that came down last winter."

"Any windows?"

"I scored two old ones at the dump. Only one pane was out. I figure I'll put one on the south and the other on the west." He scratched his beard with his thumb. "You ever install any windows like that?"

"Wood frames?"

"Yeah. I'm going to replace all the putty and repaint them."

"Not much to it. One of these days when I come up with a mess of bottom fish I'll stop over and take a look. You and Susan like snapper?"

Jack nodded. "Susan can do it Chinese."

The man in the jogging outfit came back out of the store carrying a bag of groceries. He stopped between the truck and the motorcycle and stood facing them, legs apart.

"I noticed neither of you gentlemen enrolled for classes this spring. We've scheduled a couple of new ones for the fall that you might find interesting. A comparative religions and the other has to do with existentialism. Both in the philosophy department. You might enjoy them."

Jack shook his head. "My veteran's benefits ran out. I can't afford to drive all the way in two or three nights a week for nothing."

"That's it," Tom said.

The man was angry. He shifted the bag from one arm to the other and tightened the large muscles in his thighs. He was about to respond when Tom spoke.

"Ain't it kind of windy to be jogging?" he asked, his eyes sweeping over the man from the shoes up.

"That all depends on which way you're going," the man said. He winked at Jack and walked quickly to his car. Jack looked carefully at the man's eyes. He saw how they looked before the wink and after. They were angry eyes, but they did not have the same look that he had seen in Tom's eyes.

Jack finished the beer. He smashed the can and tossed it into the box. Then he walked back into the store. He selected a six-pack of beer. When he came back outside, Tom was sitting on the fender of his truck with a beer in one hand and the half-empty package of nuts in the other. Jack crouched down and put the beer in the open saddlebag.

"His enrollment must be dropping now that most of us have used up our benefits," Tom said.

Jack swung his leg over the motorcycle and sat down. He picked up the red helmet and looked at it.

"A man starts out running with the wind, sooner or later he's gotta turn around," he said.

Tom nodded. "Then you're bucking the wind."

"That's right. You want to get back where you started, you gotta turn around. Then it's in your face. It's in your face all the way back."

Jack put the helmet on and fastened the chin strap in place. Beginning at the bottom he snapped his jacket closed until the black leather was tight against his throat. He gave Tom a brief wave and kicked down on the starter.

He left the parking lot and started back toward home. Already he could feel the wind. Leaning forward, he turned up the throttle.

ESTATE PLANNING

1

Sunday morning and I'm out alone riding my bike, thinking about my wife Gail and the fuss she makes when it comes to birthdays. Now for me, birthdays aren't that big a deal. Of course it's nice to be remembered. Nice to know you are being thought of. Some folks must go through the whole day and no one knows it's their birthday or gives a damn. Well, those are people Gail either doesn't know or doesn't care a rat's ass about.

She's got a special calendar, Gail does, a birthday calendar she keeps on the wall by her desk at the house. On this calendar the dates in a month are not wedded to the days of the week so you can refer to it year after year. On the line beside each date of each month she has written the names of the persons she cares about who celebrate their birthdays on that day. Beside the sixth day of May, for example, it says "John." So, when we came to the end of April and she flipped the page, she saw that one of the people celebrating a birthday in May was her husband.

The sixth of May was last Sunday and it wasn't just any birthday, it was my sixty-fifth. Now to me, the thirty-seventh, the sixty-fifth, what's the difference? It's a day like any other day, a number like any other number. But that's not Gail.

So when I woke up about six-thirty and headed for the john to take a whiz she called out from the bed saying, "You come back here now soon as you're finished." I hadn't even remembered yet that it was my birthday but when I heard that tone in her voice my first thought was, Okay, it's my birthday and we're going to enjoy a little pre-breakfast "snuggle."

Snuggle's the word we use for it. That's all I'm going to say. It doesn't matter if we like oral, or do it missionary or dog style, use massage oil or whips, watch porno flicks, talk dirty or sweet or never whisper a sound. It's none of your business except to know we use the word snuggle and for us the sex part of our marriage always has been and still is great.

So, I finished my business and got back in bed as instructed. She gave me a big kiss and wished me a happy birthday. Then, soon as I made a move, she called a halt. "No, no," she said, holding up a finger. "Not yet. First thing is breakfast in bed." And before I knew it she was out of the bed and standing on her feet.

I could have anything I wanted for breakfast (except the snuggle) and I was going to have it in bed, whether I wanted it there or not. She was a tad disappointed that I ordered the usual oatmeal with raisins and half a banana, a couple slices of toast, a glass of orange juice and a cup of coffee. But it was my birthday and if that's what I wanted, that's what I'd get. A few minutes later she was back with a tray. In addition to my order there was a vase holding a single flower and two cards, the envelopes sealed, my name carefully written on the outside.

Gail is big on cards. Altogether I got seven cards on my birthday. Two with the breakfast, three at random times during the day and two more when she took me out for dinner at an intimate little French place not far from the campus. The two cards on the breakfast tray were joke cards. Cards about growing older. Cards making fun of the old man. The three during the day were sweet, couples walking together along a beach holding hands, that kind of thing. The one she handed me after the waitress had taken our order was one of those expensive multi-page gismos with ruffles and affirmations of true love now and forever. When I looked up from reading it Gail had a little grin on her face and tears in her eyes. Then, after the main course and before the dessert, she pulled out my present. Gail doesn't go overboard on presents. It's the thought more than the stuff for her. But this was a small nicely wrapped package containing a pair of Lycra cycling shorts. When I held them up she whispered that I should take them to the restroom, put them on and model them for her and the other diners.

Fat chance, kid. Then the chef and the entire restaurant staff delivered a little cake with a candle and stood around the table singing Happy Birthday. (Fortunately, I don't get embarrassed all that easily.) Anyway, after all that, and after a cognac, Gail handed over the last card. This one was downright risqué, pointing us toward home and back to the bed where it had all started. When I got that card I realized that the day my wife Gail had planned for me had been one long seduction. Not a bad way to spend your sixty-fifth birthday.

But now as I descend the little hill on my bike and enter the village of Korbel I begin to think that something else had been on Gail's mind beside seduction and showing me a good time. Korbel, by the way, is a tiny place that hangs off the side of a large sawmill like a fanny pack. It being Sunday the mill is shut down and the village quiet. Riding through town feels like pedaling through a museum after it has closed and everyone has gone home.

The subject Gail brought up during our pillow talk after the snuggle and before we fell asleep had been, I now realized, the ultimate objective of her carefully and charmingly laid plans. She had learned of a seminar, she explained, a seminar being held the following night and she wanted the two of us to attend. A seminar on the lofty subject of estate planning. Tell me, what, at that point, could I say?

§

I cross the old bridge at the edge of town and stop at the base of a long hill. I pull a water bottle out of its cage and lean my bike against the grassy bank at the side of the road. I stretch my back and look around. A cool ocean fog came in overnight making the sky gray and the air still. It is a fine May morning. A fine day for a bicycle ride, a ride into new country. A ride I have fanaticized about for some time.

The seminar that I consented to while in a state of post-coital bliss took place in a sterile conference room at the Serendipity Inn located near the off ramp north of town. The coffee was bad and the cookies worse and they were the best parts of the evening. The seminar itself was presented by an out-of-town slick-suit and choreographed like one of those late-night infomercials with endless attachments and one-time-only offers while the dude droned on about annuities. He had a young assistant whose task consisted of holding up and waving around samples of the documents the guy was discussing, as if the pieces of paper had special significance in themselves even though we couldn't read a word written on them. The assistant had an air of faint embarrassment about her as if she too smelled a scam. In my frustration and boredom I had a vision of myself confined to a wheelchair, an Afghan wrapped around my useless legs. My young wife is placing a pen in my quivering fingers saying, "Happy birthday, my dear. Now sign this while you still can."

As we walked out to the parking lot afterwards, I made the following comment to Gail: "Hunter S. Thompson. Now there was an estate plan."

"What are you talking about?"

"A pistol in a drawer."

"Asshole!" she said, slamming the car door in my face.

§

I'm not proud of that exchange, by the way. I did resent Gail dragging me off to a miserable Monday evening and I do feel a vague sense of betrayal as if all the muss and fuss around the birthday had been calculated to lure me into that seminar. But the remark itself I am not proud of. At my age, I like to think I am beyond "scoring points" with comments like that. A "caustic tongue" was the term my first wife Rachel had used to describe this tendency that I apparently possessed back then. A tendency I employed when I wanted to be "hurtful" rather than "open" and "sharing," if I may rejuvenate a few of Rachel's favorite words from back in the days when our marriage was going to hell.

Still, standing now by the old bridge at Korbel, the Hunter S. Thompson quip does bring a smile to my lips. It strikes me as quite clever actually, and when you come down to it perfectly justified. Gail's timing had been atrocious. A seminar on estate planning, for Christ's sake! The very day after my sixty-fifth birthday! The whole birthday scenario planned around it? Where, I wonder, had she come up with that idea? Some ad in the local paper? Chatter at the health club with a gal on an adjacent Stairmaster, both of them marching along at seven in the morning over-fueled with lattes? A seminar presented by some out-of-town slime ball? Did she think there were no local attorneys doing this kind of work? Most of whom I know to one degree or another through my appraisal work. And hadn't we already talked about this? Hadn't I mentioned Dave Silver as a guy who had this kind of practice? A guy we could work with?

I distinctly remember that we had discussed the issue a couple of times. And, yes, I had agreed it would be a good idea to update our wills at some point. I was open to that. I had no problem with that. Our existing wills are hopelessly out of date. We signed them years before when Celeste was a toddler and Braden, my son from my first marriage, was only fourteen. Now with Celeste nineteen and just completing her first year of college all that language about guardians and someone to manage the estate was irrelevant. Were the worst to happen, Gail and I are confident that Celeste can handle whatever life places before her.

Admittedly, as to Braden there are concerns. How to fit him into the plan, that is the question. Rachel, wife number one and Braden's mother, described him in a recent phone call as troubled. Gail would, I suspect, prefer the word "devious" though she has never used that exact term with me. I agreed with Rachel that Braden was troubled, had lost his way, felt beaten down, and being in that state could, I agreed with Gail, under certain circumstances act in a devious manner. But I didn't think then, and don't think now that my son was, or is, in any way *really* devious.

The problem was Gail's timing and her urgent insistence on the seminar that annoyed me more than anything. That wheelchair vision had not been fun, and in a way I blame her for putting me through it. All that talk about physical and mental deterioration. Mr. Slick-Suit had been a self-serving town crier of bad news, spieling out fear and dread in the service of sales.

As I stand now at the foot of the Korbel hill I measure that dark wheelchair image against the man I know I am: a healthy, vigorous, sixty-five-year-old with no chronic health problems. The last time I went in for a physical the nurse asked what medications I was taking. When I said none, she seemed astonished. The expression on her face gave me something to gloat about all day.

Of course, to give Gail her due, being only forty-three herself, a sixty-fifth birthday might seem more like a milestone to her than it does to me. *"My husband is turning sixty-five!"* I can imagine that phrase rattling around in her cute head as she searched the racks for clever cards. *"My husband is old!"* As if I wasn't old yesterday but am today! The foolishness of that line of thought is self-evident to someone like myself who works with numbers all day, though it is probably less obvious to a self-confessed lover of birthdays, anniversaries and holidays who spends most of her waking hours thinking in French, this being the subject Gail teaches at the local high school.

On the other hand it is also possible, I now realize, that the milestone, if there is a milestone, measures Gail's condition more than mine. With Celeste off to college this has been the year of the empty nest coupled with her soon-to-come "time of life," as they euphemistically say, further compounded by the sudden arrival of Braden back on the scene. Whatever the cause, I have been aware for the last few weeks that Gail's usually buoyant mood has grown somewhat uneasy. A sense of foreboding tends to color her perceptions. Her exaggerated fears about Braden, this sudden urgency for an estate plan, to give but two examples.

§

The water in the bottle is cool and refreshing. I pull out an energy bar, tear open the wrapper and bite a chunk off the corner. I glance at my watch and then the odometer. Nine o'clock. I have been on the road for about an hour and have gone thirteen casual mostly flat miles. My average speed was 12.5 and I wasn't pushing it. I have a long way to go but I'm not out of breath. My legs feel strong. I have just gotten warmed up.

Rudy, my late father, comes to mind as I chew. Not to my mind, I'm thinking, but to Gail's. It seemed reasonable that my birthday should have brought Rudy into to her fertile mind, an unwanted popup ad featuring Rudy as this rude medieval peasant who stands in her doorway threatening to step in and soil her carpet. Gail never could stomach the old factory worker. Not that I blame her. From the beginning Rudy saw Gail as a whore and though he made feeble efforts to hold his tongue his underlying opinion never wavered. Nothing personal, really, that was more or less Rudy's definition of a second wife, any second wife, especially a younger one. And to Gail, Rudy always seemed not simply barbaric but ancient, he being almost thirty years older than Al, her own father. Al, the absent somewhat idealized daddy, the literary down-on-his-luck-and-dead-at-fifty, Al.

"At that angle you remind me of Rudy," she has of late been known to observe. I don't take it as a compliment.

§

Standing on the south side of Korbel this Sunday morning chewing an energy bar and enjoying the open air, I decide that I am happy to be alone on this ride. Alone, however, was not my first choice. I am alone because my friend Steve Grogon refused to join me. Steve, along with the other gray-hairs in our cycling group, will be starting out about now on our normal Sunday ride. That ride goes north along the coast, twenty miles up and twenty back with decent pavement, most of it level, a mocha and a bagel at the turnaround, a prevailing tailwind to push you home.

But to honor my sixty-fifth birthday I wanted to try something more challenging. Earlier in the week

I decided to attempt the Loop. It would be a birthday present to myself. A secret birthday present because I hadn't mentioned my plans to Gail. She is out of town picking Celeste up from school and enjoying a girls-only Mother's Day weekend in the city. Given her mood of late I saw no reason to worry her.

The Loop is a famous ride among local cyclists. At forty-seven miles it's not much longer than our normal Sunday ride, but it takes you back into remote and rugged ranch and timberland. It's strenuous enough that cyclists who ride centuries use it for training. You need to carry two bottles of water, a good supply of food, tools, a tube or two and a patch kit. Much of the road is terrible, some of it gravel. A lot of it is up. There are two major climbs. The first, which I am standing at the base of now, climbs over a thousand feet in two and a half miles through a series of turns. The road surface on the hill is paved, but lumpy and broken, particularly at the bottom, and the grade will be steepest at the top where I will be least prepared to handle it. That's what I've been told. I have driven the route in a car but never tried to ride it. As to the second climb, well, I'm not going to think about that now.

Steve Grogon tried to talk me out of this little adventure. According to him I was crazy to try the Loop alone. He might be willing to accompany me at some later date, he said, but he wanted us to complete a strenuous two-month training program first. Steve is an organized, careful, hard-science, kind of guy. He emailed me a spread sheet which I translated as follows: continue our Sunday rides but extend them in weekly five-mile intervals to sixty miles along with other shorter rides as time permits. Add spin classes two days a week at the local health club, the one where Gail does her Stairmaster gig. Meanwhile, he wrote, we would need to get lots of rest and good nutrition. He even sent along some suggestions as to diet and an itemization of what supplies we should take on the ride. Two months of that regimen and he might be willing to join me. Maybe our wives, he proposed, could follow us in a van filled with tools and supplies, a van large enough to carry both bikes and both bodies home if things didn't work out.

Gee, Steve, I thought when I read that, sure you don't want a Medevac team hovering overhead?

That's what I thought. What I shot back was: "Steve, I'm going this weekend. By myself if necessary."

"Sorry to hear that. I think you're making a mistake."

I climb on my bike. I shift into a low gear and I start up the hill.

2

I have no reason to hurry. Being alone I feel no pressure to keep up with the peloton. And with Gail and Celeste entertaining themselves in the city, I don't have to imagine my family sitting at home worrying.

Traffic is minimal; I can weave about the roadway looking for the smoothest course, avoiding the multiple potholes and bulges in the asphalt. The mounds of asphalt remind me of the hives that suddenly popped out on Braden's skin one night when he was visiting us as a teenager. They were all over him, arms, legs, belly and back. The thin pale boy came into the kitchen that morning, naked but for his white briefs, a look of horror on his face, his hairless body quivering. Gail, seated at the breakfast table nursing Celeste, ordered Braden to leave the room immediately, thinking the kid was the carrier of some vicious contagion. "And get yourself dressed," she yelled toward the retreating child. "Your father is taking you to the emergency room."

The hives were mostly gone by the time we reached the hospital and so far as I know have never returned. But what do I know? They could have come back. They could have returned a dozen times and I wouldn't know. After the breakup the boy was raised on the East Coast by his mother with annual two-week visits out here.

That night as we were driving home from the seminar, Gail said, "John, we really *do* need to think about this stuff. We *do* need a plan. A real plan."

"You're right, we'll do a plan." I was coming to regret the Hunter Thompson quip. Clever, yes, but regrettable. It wasn't Gail's fault the guy had been a slime-ball.

"You say that, but you don't do anything about it. You said you were going to talk to Dave Silver. That was weeks ago. I've asked five or six times: Have you talked to Dave? And you haven't. You still haven't."

"I haven't had a chance, I tell you, but I will. I've known Dave for years. He's a good lawyer and he does this stuff all the time. Not like that clown."

It was well after dark and the fog was thick and low. I wanted to reach over and caress my wife's thigh but I felt obliged to keep both hands securely attached to the wheel. The lights from the approaching cars were blinding. That is something I've noticed of late. I'm becoming less comfortable driving at night.

Gail went on talking: "If we don't have a plan, one of us will be left with a mess, you know that. And if we both went at the same time? Like on a plane or something? I shudder to think. You heard what that guy said. If we both died without a plan Braden gets half of everything you own!"

Gail had carefully asked Mr. Slick-Suit that question. Soon as he opened it up for questions, hers was the first hand in the air. Good teacher, good student.

"Okay, we'll do a plan." I was trying to focus on the traffic. It's those damn huge pickups they're driving these days. The headlights are flat-out aggressive. They come at you like machines of war. And you know who's driving them, I was thinking, guys on drugs, guys on booze. Some clown who's just had a brawl with his girlfriend. Half of them probably have a weapon stowed in the glove compartment.

"Can you imagine the kind of pressure he would put on her?"

"Who?"

"Who? Braden, of course. Are you listening at all?"

"Gail, we need a plan. I acknowledge that. How many times do I have to say it? You're right. We need a plan. And I haven't gotten on it as fast as I should, all right?"

I hoped that this outburst contained the requisite amounts of admission, confession and remorse. Ingredients belonging on the spice rack of every spouse, as over the years I have slowly and painfully come to learn. Which is not to suggest insincerity. I meant what I said. On the other hand, given the small fortune we had just shelled out for Celeste's first year in college and knowing that three or more years lay ahead, I wasn't, truth be told, eager to pay a lawyer two or three grand just to set up something I didn't think we needed all that urgently. According to Slick-Suit a simple will no longer cuts the mustard. No, we need a trust. We need sheaths of documents. We need a whole plan. And it won't come cheap.

Gail was quiet for a moment but then she said, "Do you know how old you are?"

"Of course I know how old I am. What kind of question is that?"

"You are almost half way between my dad's age when he died and the age Rudy was when he died. Think about that."

I thought about that. My wife's logic eluded me but I dutifully ran the numbers. Al, Gail's old man, had been taken out at fifty by pancreatic cancer. He felt a pain while seated at his desk in the miserable little store in Portland where he sold used books and old vinyl albums and it was downhill from there. In my mind you can forget the decades of cigar smoke, the drugs and the other vices Al had put himself through in his determination to be bohemian. What I most remember was that store in Portland. It has always seemed to me that if musty can kill it was musty that got Al.

But even accepting Gail's bizarre thesis—that since I was as many years older than her father at the time of his death as I was younger than my father at the time of his, that my own croaking was therefore likely at any minute—I still had a couple of years to go before I reached the halfway point. Rudy, after all, made it to eighty-four. Most of which he spent eating bacon for breakfast, ham for lunch and sausage for dinner while engaging in nothing more strenuous than mowing the lawn a couple of times a month, scooping out the occasional snow drift (later he got a snow blower) and punching the remote to make sure he didn't miss a single professional wrestling match. But rather than question Gail's reasoning or her math, I thought I'd be generous.

"*Dead* center," I acknowledged.

"John, that is not funny."

I agreed. It wasn't funny. About this subject nothing is funny.

§

I climb the hill seated, spinning away in the granny gears, the smallest of the triple in front, the outsized largest in the rear. The country is already feeling remote, scrub timber, glimpsed views back down into the valley. I pass no structures and see only two vehicles, both rumbling, workaday pickups. That's why you do it on a Sunday, the very fit woman at the cycling shop had advised me: no logging trucks. I watch my odometer with an obsession that I know to be somewhat foolish, counting each tenth of a mile a triumph. A mile up from the bridge I stop for water and another chunk of energy bar.

Gail is going through changes, I'm thinking when I start out again. A few months ago that Hunter Thompson barb would have bounced off harmlessly. She might have given tooth for claw as it were, responding with a wisecrack of her own, or in the alternative dismissed me with something like "Clever, John," one of her favorites, meaning, of course, the opposite.

And, had I let loose with that crack not one but twenty years earlier, back when Gail and I met, she the lovely new French teacher starting her first job out of college, me the distinguished forty-five-year-old professional serving his first term on the school board—well, back then she would have erupted in bright unrestrained laughter, tears of delight glistening at the corners of her eyes. She used to *read* Hunter S. Thompson, for Christ's sake! In French!

At least that's the way I remember her during those crisp days the autumn we met. An autumn that followed a cold and dismal fog-gray summer during which my marriage to Rachel had fractured like lake ice before an icebreaker. Propriety required, of course, that I resign from the school board a short time later. It was a position I had campaigned for (my only effort at public office) and won the previous spring. During the campaign I had presented myself as the responsible father of Braden, then in the fifth grade, and the loving husband of Rachel, whom everyone knew as the yoga teacher who attended PTA meetings in tights and advocated for the elimination of all forms of sugar from school grounds. Now a few months later I was the old man banging the new French teacher while my wife stood around plucking at her leggings, red-eyed and enraged.

The divorce became final the next summer and Gail and I got married a few days later. An act which, coupled with my resignation, allowed Gail to remain on staff. She really is a great teacher and no one wanted to get rid of her, but....

§

With the mill closed and quiet below me and there being no wind, the only sounds come from my own breathing, from the rattle of the bike on the rough surface punctuated by a rhythmic click from where the cleat of my right shoe locks onto the pedal. "You can't call climbing this hill fun," I say out loud, "but I'm doing all right."

By the time Gail and I got hooked, Rachel and Braden had fled to Philadelphia where years before Rachel's mother had herself fled, she to distance herself from Rachel's father who was on faculty at Cornell and according to family legend, a legendary scoundrel. About the truth of that purported scandal I know nothing. Rachel's parents' marriage had broken up some time before I met Rachel. My only sighting of the alleged scoundrel occurred at our wedding where I seem to remember him as a handsome fellow hovering always close to the drinks' table.

I do have reason, however, to question the truth of the charges made against this man, seeing as how that family has laid charges against me. I can state with complete certainty that my marriage to Rachel did not break up because of Gail. The marriage was over before I even met her. But according to Braden, Rachel's mother, though perhaps not Rachel herself, relates a different tale. In the mother's version Rachel and I hadn't really broken up when Gail and I got together; Rachel and I were going through a brief separation, a sort of summer camp experience you might say, brought on by my obsession with work, and that we had planned to get back together again in the fall.

Recalling this juicy slander sends me pedaling a bit faster up the hill.

Braden refuses to have an opinion on the issue, incidentally, or if he has one, has wisely refused to express it. Gail, however, has long suspected that Braden is an operative for Rachel. That he secretly believes that his stepmother destroyed his cozy childhood by stealing me away, leaving him and his mother abandoned and bereft.

Personally, I didn't think anyone including Braden or Rachel gives a good damn about any of this. Rachel remarried and appears quite content, or at least was until things started getting weird with Braden.

§

My eyes are still reflexively watching the odometer as I approach the second mile and a second rest stop well earned. That's when I become aware of a new sound. I turn my head thinking it's coming from the trees somewhere to my right. Amazingly, and irrationally, my first thought is that somewhere in the middle distance a bongo player is wandering through the steep woods stoned on mushrooms. The sound is rhythmic, all right, loud and pronounced. Could it be a woodpecker? Not so. The bongo, it turns out, is being pounded from the inside. The old ticker, as Rudy used to say, and my chest has become a drumhead.

I stop. I pull off my helmet. I try to breathe deep and low against the diaphragm. I drink some water. Then as the pounding subsides I become aware of how quiet it is. No cars, no wind, no airplane overhead. No jet skis, no leaf blowers, no car alarms, no chainsaws, no asshole closing a stock deal on his cell phone…. I am alone in the world standing on a hillside straddling my bike.

I look back toward the valley and a breath of air presses against my jersey. The damp cloth feels deliciously cold against my chest and stomach. A movement now causes me to glance up and I catch sight of a raven gliding down just above the conifers following the bends in the road. It navigates with minute adjustments of its wings and tail feathers, and passes silently over my head. I take another bite of energy bar.

The assent is steep when I resume, steep enough that even in the lowest gear I am punishing my knees. The old knees. The knees that had forced me to give up jogging not long after I met Gail. After that I did walking, then swimming, then rowing and finally cycling. Cycling seems to strengthen the knees, but only if I do it right.

Don't rush, I tell himself now. That's the temptation: to get to the top and end the pain.

The stress on the knees reminds me of Gail's recent suggestion that we move to a smaller house. Celeste is mostly gone now. We should keep a room free for her but we don't need all the extra space, the large yard. Gail thinks we should have a garage sale and pare down. She also thinks I should cut back on work with an eye toward retirement. With her teaching schedule we could do more traveling if I wasn't working so much. She wants to get back to France where she had been an exchange student two or three times and has visited on a number of occasions since. Not go for a week or two she was suggesting. Go there. Find a place and settle in for a while.

Gail's understanding of our economic situation, it seems to me, has been shaped by twenty years of monthly paychecks. The school district has been underfunded for years. The finances grow ever more dire, causing the suggestion to resurface now and then that French be dropped from the curriculum entirely. Still, every month a paycheck settles with deft electronic precision into her account. And with each payment her retirement benefits wax a little fatter. This experience has given Gail a sense of comfort that does not exist for me, that seems vaguely delusional to me. At my office the phone has to keep ringing. People have to call seeking my services or no money makes its way into my account. Yes, we have investments. But how much will we need? How long will we live? How much care will we require? In this economy can you count on anything long term? Once I turn off the faucet nothing more will come out the pipe.

Besides, I like appraising real estate. I like the contact with people, deadlines, obligations. Truth be told, I am a plodder by nature. "I do what I do and I keep doing what I'm doing," was a self-assessment I offered to Gail not long ago, bringing a baffled expression to her face. Admittedly, the sentiment so stated will not likely to find its way into Bartlett's book of great quotations. But it is true. Take right now. I have found a rhythm and I am staying with it. Who but a plodder would be fool enough to climb this hill on a bicycle? There's lots of flat land and smooth road. It's not like you can't get exercise on the flat, assuming it's exercise you're after.

Finally, as I near the summit, the forest gives way to a patch of sloping range land. Earlier, as I was riding out of town, I passed a number of what Canadians call hobby farms, small spreads with brightly painted barns, neat white fences, a horse or two grazing near the road. The hobby farms are now far behind me. I have reached the bottom edge of a working ranch. The outbuildings, the fencing, the chutes and troughs are gray, bare-boarded slack-looking and functional.

On one side of the road a lone bull stands near the fence nosing his morning ration of alfalfa. He's black, mature, thick, dusty, still. One horn curls in as if deformed and on his flank near the base of his tail the number 0114 has been neatly etched in dirty white. Across the road a woman in her forties, also thick, is forking chunks of loose alfalfa from the bed of a pickup to a dozen or so cows. I can smell the hay and the animals as I pass. The woman grunts an acknowledgment of my little wave. I lack the breath to say anything.

3

A hundred or so yards beyond the cattle and the diligent cattlewoman, the road forks. The left branch continues climbing up through the ranch and on toward still higher country. Tales have come to me of riders who dare go in that direction but they play in a league beyond mine. I veer right and am soon plunged back into patchy logged-over timber.

There is something about having reached the top of an obstacle by your own power that is intoxicating. As I bounce along the lousy asphalt, joy-juices begin to flood through my bloodstream. Yes, my legs feel limp as warm rubber, but my God, I think, look at this wild country, at the remote vitality of it. "Eat your heart out, Steve Grogon," I shout, "you have no idea what you're missing!"

I have become the person I most truly am: a soul set loose in the world, free to wander about searching for grace. This epiphany leads to an idea that seems wildly inspired. Not tonight probably because Gail and Celeste will be tired from their long drive back from the city, but Monday after work I'll pile them in the car and drive them over the Loop. I'll point out the sights I'm seeing now, the hills I'm climbing, the terrain I'm covering. I'll show them what it means to be sixty-five, vital, healthy and alive. Seeing this country, seeing what I've accomplished will bring comfort to Gail. From the back seat Celeste will be patting my shoulder, kissing my neck, wildly impressed.

I realize now, what I had been only dimly aware of before: I am on this ride because of Gail. Look, my dear young wife, it's just a number! We have years, good years, ahead of us.

And Braden! Maybe I can persuade him to come along. The whole family bunched together in the car. When he was a toddler, two, maybe a little more, Braden loved to have Rachel and me set up treasure hunts for him in the living room. He would be a determined little man, running about poking his head under the chairs, lifting up pillows, opening drawers, laughing and yelling. Watching him in his sweater and his baggy corduroy pants you got the impression that in Braden's mind the thing he was searching for, the candy kiss, the tiny toy, was actively hiding from him. That it might sneak from one place to another the moment he turned his head. That the object he was seeking was having as much fun as he was.

I have no idea where that child has gone. What remains is a balding man in his thirties, seemingly lost in a funk. Maybe Braden has decided that the thing he was searching for, whatever it was, has proven itself too wily, too smart for him. But sitting in the backseat beside Celeste, seeing what I have accomplished, might he not recapture some of that childhood joy, that enthusiasm, that *will* to try, that determination to see things through? Might it not inspire him to climb on a bike himself? Cycling, of course! Why hadn't I thought of that before? We will start slow, build up his strength and endurance. I will help him get the right equipment, the right fit so he's comfortable. No unnecessary pain. The idea is to have fun out there. Soon he'll be joining us old guys on the Sunday ride, a new man, a new Braden.

About this time a tiny alarm begins to sound in my skull. Its message is simple: the euphoria you are experiencing, sir, is not a sensation you can trust. You have more than thirty miles still to cover. Right now you need to think about the next ten of them. It will be bad road, sir, all of it. There will be little climbs that sap your strength. It will twist and descend until it eventually delivers you to the banks of Maple Creek. Then it will take you along the valley to the bridge that crosses the river. And from the river, sir….

Yes, I understand. From the river I will have to start climbing all over again.

Sobriety, instantly restored.

§

"What would we do in Europe?" I asked Gail over cocktails the other night.

"Do there?"

"Yeah. You know, after a while. You look at a few cathedrals, you visit a few castles, art museums, you shop, you eat in restaurants. But what would we *do*?"

"I can't believe you're asking that question," she said.

But she saw it; she recognized I was putting her on, and the memory of the glint that came into her eyes makes me laugh out loud. My God, I do love that woman. Quick as a whip, she is. Loved her from the start and I love her now. Nothing else matters, really. You can take your careful calculations and throw it out the door when it comes to this kind of thing. So what I was a forty-five-year-old real estate agent with a son, an estranged wife and a reputation in the community. So what she was a twenty-two-year-old college graduate with a sort of boyfriend back in France starting a new career in a new town where she wanted to present herself in the best possible light. None of that mattered. There was just the energy, the passion, the giggling intense rush of it. The idea that we should have or could have turned away was ludicrous.

A couple miles beyond the fork I stop. I am standing below a ranch house set high on the sloping hip of a grassy hill. The spread appears occupied but there is no one about that I can see. I know the house in a superficial way. I've never appraised it, but years before when I was still selling real estate I did a walk-through with a dozen other realtors. Nothing unique or particularly interesting about its layout or design, so far as I can recall, but the view is spectacular. And from when I drove the route, I know that this house is the only building I will see, this grassy hill one of the few openings in the forest that I will pass between the fork behind me and the next ranch miles below on the banks of the creek.

The fog feels lower here. It hides everything in the distance, obliterating the view I so fondly remember. But I know where I am. I'm perched on the eastern side of a deep cleavage formed by the river and its tributaries. To the west, miles away as the crow flies, is a series of hills that leads to the second summit and the road that delivers me back to town. Before me, a few yards away, the meadow ends and the narrow strip of asphalt descends back into the trees.

I promised myself before I left home that I would do an assessment at this point. I need to honestly determine whether I should turn around here or go the distance. The choice has to be made now. Once I reach the valley floor it will be too late. Down there, if I turn back or go ahead, the distance home will be roughly the same, and either way out is up. I can hear Steve Grogon comforting me on our next ride. "So, you turned back, John. No shame in that. You did climb the Korbel hill on a bike, man. How many sixty-five-year-olds can say that?"

I pull a wedge of orange from the plastic bag in my pouch. I put the whole thing in my mouth, grab a corner of the rind with my fingers and pull, peeling the precious fruit free with my teeth. I drink water. I finish off the first energy bar. I take out a second wedge of orange. By the time I reach the trees I'm clutching the brakes.

§

My mind goes back to Gail and Braden. Her fears about him are, it seems to me, exaggerated but deeply felt. It's a long-standing, deeply ingrained problem. As a new stepmother she had tried too hard, wanting badly to establish a bond, knowing instinctively that I was more likely to leave her for Braden than I was for Rachel. Not yet twenty-five and starting a new career, Gail had probably not given thought one to being a parent, much less a stepmother to an emotionally fragile thirteen-year-old boy. The age factor was particularly challenging. She was, by a decade, closer in age to my son than she was to me. The temptation had to be overwhelming. Braden already had a mother; she would become his big sister, his friend, his contemporary.

For his part, Braden resented and distrusted her. Her advances must have struck him as fawning, fraudulent and somehow sinister. And being the age he was, the little animal inside almost certainly experienced both guilt and constant lust whenever he saw her. I feel a sudden rush of sympathy for both of them and the positions they found themselves in. At the time, I had a clumsy sense of both her desperation and his resistance and I fell into the role of the hapless placater. I was the fool with the stupid grin, wanting everyone to have fun, filling them with ice cream and candy, organizing games, taking them on trips to movies and game parks, whatever it took to cover the chasm with an illusion of harmony.

Shared custody had been a nightmare. Gail and Rachel could barely look at each other and remain civil. Each exchange of physical possession involved a negotiation, flesh was demanded and sold. Braden felt shuttled back and forth, two houses but no home. Rachel's decision to finally take Braden and return to the East Coast brought both relief and profound grief. Gail pushed for a quick marriage. Then for a child. Only when she became pregnant with Celeste, it seems to me, did my young wife truly relax.

The pregnancy had terrified me. I had seen a marriage go sour. I had lost a child and I had no stomach for reliving that particular nightmare. But Gail had been right, her instincts true as often they are. The birth of our sweet, bright daughter brought a sense of calm to everyone. I had a new child to adore. Gail now had a second bond with me. Rachel remarried and ended up having another child herself. Braden settled into school in Philadelphia and seemed to get along with his stepfather. I gave up selling real estate and turned to appraising it, freeing my weekends to be with my new family. Gail took three years off to be a full-time mom and then returned to teaching.

I am having trouble seeing the road all of a sudden. Tears well up in my eyes. I have truly become an old fool but I can't help it. The thought of Celeste, sweet child, and what she had done for all of us just by innocently coming into the world strikes me now as an act of great charity.

§

Every summer Braden came out for two weeks in July or August. He loved his baby sister and she him. We tried to do things together as a family. But Gail was now a mother. She could play the role with either child and Braden was a sloppy, forgetful kid who liked to sleep in, who left clothes lying about, who tended to drop precious objects on hard surfaces. Each year a new Braden would show up. He could be awkward, acned. He could be funny, charming, sullen or withdrawn. One summer he only wanted to play basketball. The camping trip we had planned he found boring and stupid. He couldn't wait to get back to the playground so he could work on his jump shot. His one goal in life was to play in the NBA. When he arrived the next year I had hung a backboard and hoop off the garage. The present brought a surprise to both of us. Braden had no interest anymore in basketball; now it was sports he thought stupid. The year he turned seventeen Gail caught him smoking marijuana in his room. The few times I got him to talk, Braden's dreams struck me as wildly unrealistic. One year he wanted to become an actor yet he seemed uneasy communicating much with anyone. When Braden did open up I thought I saw a vulnerability that was painful to look into. He did, however, possess a comic sense that could and regularly did send Celeste into hysterics, usually just before bedtime. Years later Celeste would take advantage of the backboard with its faded paint and the basket with its tattered net. She played on the basketball team all through high school.

The visits and the child support ended when Braden turned eighteen. Our family flew back to Philadelphia for his high school graduation, a weekend of cautious civility and shared discomfort. We went again for Braden's marriage at the age of twenty-two to a divorced woman six years his senior, a disaster that ended five months later. After that he attended a clown school, partially on my dime, an act of generosity that Gail resented and still brings up now and then. For a while he worked in a bookstore that, though I never saw it, I imagined as not unlike the one that had killed off old Al.

Then last winter Rachel called. We had exchanged Christmas cards but it had been years since I had spoken with her on the phone. She was calling about Braden, she said.

"I see." I feared the worst.

"He's lost his job again."

"The bookstore?"

"The bookstore? John, Braden hasn't worked in a bookstore for years."

"I didn't know."

"No, I suppose not. He says you never call. Sales, he was in sales, shoes mostly, but in this economy."

"I see."

"Anyway he got laid off, that's the important thing. Then he couldn't make his car payments and the bank...."

"Couldn't you help him on that?" I inserted without thinking.

The yoga teacher lost it then. "What do you think we've been doing for the last five years! And what have you done!"

"I'm sorry."

My God, John. He's not Bill's son. He's yours."

"I understand. But you mean he's ours don't you? Yours and mine. And he's hardly a kid. He's thirty… almost." All of a sudden I couldn't remember my son's exact age.

Rachel sighed. "He's thirty-three. Your son is thirty-three."

"He should've called. I could've sent him a few bucks. So he has no car?"

"No car, no job, no apartment, no girlfriend, no prospects. He's back here living upstairs."

"Oh my."

"He brings his laundry down and shows up regularly for meals. I'm worried about him, John. I'm afraid he might do something, you know, to himself. And Bill has had it up to his eyebrows."

"Oh my," I said again.

"He doesn't need a few bucks. He's your son and he needs a fresh start."

Years had passed since I had been in regular communication with my first wife but I felt myself sliding into a familiar groove. I knew exactly what Rachel was about to suggest.

"I don't know that we could do that…," I started to say.

"I know Gail won't be…."

"Yes. And Celeste is in college now. The cost is mind-boggling...."

"I understand. But Braden has always talked a lot about the times he spent with you. Both before and after our divorce...."

"I didn't know."

"He admires you greatly, and he loves Celeste!"

Everybody loves Celeste, I said to myself.

"Oh my," I said one more time to Rachel.

§

I have entered the most remote and the least maintained stretch of the ride. I cannot take my eyes off the road for more than a second. The pavement is jarring and unpredictable. I think my tire pump might dislodge, that the water bottles might pop from their cages. Sometimes the pavement disappears entirely and I find myself bouncing over gravel. My shoulders and elbows, the palms of my gloved hands all feel bruised. I have to constantly adjust to maintain my balance. Pushing against both sides of the road are stands of recovering forest. Near the road itself, the ground beneath the trees is covered with poison oak, its foliage coated with grayish road dust. Timber company land. Now and then a dirt road leads off into the trees, its entrance blocked by a locked steel gate.

I come upon a recent clearcut and then, rounding a curve, a second. The earth is exposed, ravaged. Raw stumps jut from the hillside amid the scattered debris of branch and bark. Visions of desolation segue to thoughts of death and my son and then on to mountain lions lurking in the brush. The population is growing, sightings becoming more frequent. Last week's newspaper had a report about two women hiking at the edge of town. A young male lion had appeared from nowhere. It circled swatting at them as they made their panicked way to the nearest house. Here there is no "nearest house." Here there is nothing and no one for miles. Then Steve Grogon, trying to be helpful, had emailed me a story about a mountain biker found dead in a Southern California park. A lion had apparently dropped onto this poor fellow from an overhanging boulder. The article hinted that the cyclist had still been alive as his liver was being devoured. Hard working guys, those mountain lions. No middleman. No long-haul supplier. No shrink-wrapped by-the-pound boneless. No freezer in the garage. Just out here day after day after day stalking living things, killing and eating them.

I move to the center of the road and pedal on. Sounds come at me from both sides. Sounds that I hope come from lizards scurrying in the duff, from fir cones tumbling through branches to land on the dry forest floor.

4

My late and second father-in-law, Musty Al, was about the same age as me, which at the time seemed a curious twist, and the occasion for some acquaintances, Rachel included, to try their hand at amateur psychoanalysis. Al was a Francophile and a poet, and the musty store he called home was named Baudelaire's. The first time I met the man he asked how much older I was than his only daughter. I stiffened, thinking I was in for a scolding. "Only twenty-two years?" he responded. The news seemed a relief to him. Baudelaire's father, he told me, had been thirty-four years older than his mother.

Gail's mother, Marty, also in my age range, never married Al, and Gail was seven before she met him. Still Gail got her love for all things French from Al and it is he, I suspect, who from the grave is pushing her to persuade her tagalong husband to cut back on this silly work business and head off to France. Celeste is a co-conspirator in all this, by the way, not quite calculating that from my office comes a good part of the cash flowing into her account and out through her debit card.

It was an honest question, I think now, teasing or not: What would we do there? And what about the mess we'd leave behind? Meaning, among other things, Braden.

My wife said, "No way is that man going to move into my house at his age!"

"That man? He's my son."

"Your thirty-four-year-old son."

"Thirty-three," I corrected confidently, having been previously corrected by Rachel.

But yes, a late age, I conceded, to begin, or to give myself a modicum of credit, resume, parenting one's child. Still, I needed to make some effort, I thought, which means, as it almost always does, spend some money. So, I flew Braden out, set him up in an apartment and bought him an operating vehicle. We called it a loan.

§

Why I was doing this was unclear to me and to everyone else except Rachel. Rachel thought it "only fair," she having examined, I presume, some ancient tally sheet maintained in a secret drawer in her boudoir along with a few tarnished pieces of silver and some bits of yellowed ivory.

Guilt, I suppose, which has a half-life longer than a human life, but there is also duty and that greeting-card thing called love. I look at my son and what I feel is what I call love in one of its many forms. I feel pleasure and pride when things go right for him and pain and shame when they go badly. I enjoy seeing him and hearing what he has to say and giving him a hug and wishing him well. Because, you see, he's mine.

Gail was hesitant but not unsympathetic. Like the rest of us she has territorial interests, her home, her daughter, the family's assets, but she also understood, and even, she said, admired, my impulse to help. What Steve Grogon called when I discussed it with him, my desire to "reinvest" in Braden.

The family debate pivots around whether a particular action will help or hurt. How much do you give and how far do you go. What encourages and what discourages initiative. Even, when do you "give up" and what does "give up" mean. Who decides when you've reached the "giving up" point? And if you think this is just "your problem" think again because this is "our home" and "our family." It's "our lives" and "our savings" you are talking about.

And just who, I think now, knows the answers to any of this? Certainly I don't.

§

Shortly after he arrived, I offered Braden a position at my office. I thought the idea brilliant to tell the truth. He could learn a skill under his father's watchful eye. In time he would become a partner. It's not brains he's lacking. He has the ability to do the work and the business is a going concern. It has a reputation and a client base and provides a steady income. One day he could take over. Then Gail and I would be free to go touring through Burgundy.

I tried this case before two separate judges and both ruled against me. Braden said it would be "weird," he may have used "kinky," to work for his dad. His eyes said he couldn't work for me because he would fail and the failure would break both his heart and mine, and of course that look caused as much, if not more, breakage than trying and failing would have. But I may have been wrong about that as well. Maybe what I thought I saw wasn't there at all. Maybe he just doesn't want to work for the old man or do the kind of work the old man does.

For her part, Gail was annoyed that I had naively proposed the idea to Braden before I discussed it with her. Suddenly, it appeared, the appraisal business was "our" business, not just "mine." She had even considered, she revealed, that one day Celeste might take over the office herself. "Given this economy, who knows what she might have to turn to make ends meet?"

"'Have to turn to?'" I shouted back, feeling a sudden rage. "'Have to turn' to appraising? So, what's wrong with appraising real estate? You act like I'm selling myself to strangers in the men's room of an interstate rest stop."

Gail didn't even look up. "Get a grip, John," she said, casually blowing a breath of air across her morning coffee. She teaches in a public high school. Nothing can phase her.

Braden, meanwhile, has been working on his magic skills, card tricks mostly. He wants to start a little business, he explained, where he would entertain kids and others at birthday parties and such. A sort of clown-magician combo from what I can make of it. In the meantime, he's found part-time work at a local casino, bussing tables in the bar-restaurant. Minimum wage but there's room to move up. They might even want him to do a magic act on their stage, he told me, once his routine is more polished.

Hearing this Gail said, "Magic shows for kids' birthday parties. Now there's a moneymaker."

Still, I was impressed by what I saw as Braden's initiative. I called Rachel to give her the happy news.

"Uh, oh," she clucked.

"Uh, oh?"

"It's not good he's that close to booze."

"No?"

"Or the slots. He's had problems with both."

§

Sometime after ten as I'm crossing a particularly treacherous stretch of gravel, concerned for my stability, the sun breaks through the morning fog. The damp closed-in feeling seems to lift. I become aware of birds fluttering in the brush. The air feels cool and clean. Not long thereafter I reach the valley floor and the pavement improves. I spot a barn that I remembered from the drive and a few minutes later pass a couple walking beside the road. Seeing them is a shock. I had somehow convinced myself I was in the middle of nowhere, but here they are enjoying a morning stroll a few hundred yards from their front door and maybe forty minutes by car from my own.

About eleven I arrive at the bridge that spans the river. I cross over and lean my bike against a post on the far side.

It's getting hot. I've traveled twenty-seven miles, considerably less than the normal Sunday ride, but I feel a little unstable on my feet, a sailor back on land after a long time at sea. To steady myself I walk back and forth across the bridge, glancing over the side at the tidy little family drama being staged below.

On the rocky beach a few yards upstream a man and a woman stand in swimsuits. They have just shoved an inflatable kayak with two young girls off into a wide calm stretch of water. The woman stands at the water's edge and yells with seeming alarm, "Chantele, are you comfortable?"

"Mom!"

"Chantele, are you all right?"

"Mom! Would you stop?"

The man ignores both her and the children. He busies himself putting away the pump he used to inflate the kayak. I understand that man. I see into his soul in a flash. As emotions swirl around him he seeks shelter for himself by performing a useful but purely physical task.

Personally, I mow the lawn. The large one Gail thinks we should get rid of. "Why are you out there pushing?" Steve Grogon asked me. "Get yourself a ride-around." It's the plodder again, caught in the act. He starts in one corner and mows the whole damn thing.

I lean against the guard rail. I eat the last two wedges of orange and then lifting the plastic bag to my lips allow the precious dribble of lingering juice to roll onto my tongue. The banana is gone. One water bottle is empty. I'm halfway through the second energy bar.

The woman's fear of disaster reminds me of the seminar and something Mr. Slick-Suit said: "We go through life being afraid of death but most of us end up living longer than we want." He was pitching long-term care insurance at that point.

"Chantele," the woman yells, "be careful!"

An image of my Aunt Catherine enters my mind. Catherine is the lone surviving relative of my parents' generation. Ninety-five and in a nursing home. "I wish I were dead," she reports regularly on the phone.

Musty Al is dead. Gone the way of all flesh has Al. From the desk drawer in the old bookstore Gail removed his stack of poems. These she lovingly assembled in a book she had privately printed. The poems are a tad scatological for my taste, and scattered throughout like fly droppings are French words and phrases that leave me lost. But some people find meaning in Al's poems, even a harsh beauty.

A few months following his death, Gail organized a memorial service in Portland. I felt quite noble, to tell the truth, tolerating with little complaint this extravagant waste of time and money for no purpose, and not a little embarrassed for Gail knowing in my heart that not a soul would show up. Wrong again!

Come they did, women in skirts that touched the floor, young men, their necks wrapped in scarves, old guys with accents and tobacco-stained facial hair who wore tattered sport coats and carried a newspaper trapped beneath one arm.

Live on, I think, staring absently at the kayak. Live on and hopefully learn. What else can you do?

5

I am twenty miles from home. The second summit is ten miles away and more than two thousand feet above me. Riders I talked to never failed to describe how pumped they had felt, and thus I would feel, when the summit is topped. They told how if I dared I could coast a full mile from that point without turning a pedal. Touch the brakes only if absolutely necessary, they warned. To make the mile you'll need to fly through a couple of blind curves, so listen close for cars. Following that first mile will be a series of rolling hills and then about six miles from home I will top a rise and a promised panorama will open before me. A thousand or more feet below I will see the bay, sailboats like specks of tissue on the water, and beyond that the ocean itself. The temperature will instantly drop ten or fifteen degrees. From then on it will be a party, three more rolling miles followed by the final brake-clutching, road-twisting, heavily-trafficked descent that will deliver me at last to the front door of our humble abode and its well-mowed lawn.

What a prospect, I'm thinking. To be immersed in cool ocean air. To hear it roaring in my ears, to feel it whipping at my jersey. To know it is all downhill from here. That I have earned this breath-taking final descent, have paid for it with sweat and pain, and have the right to enjoy it without reservation. The joy! The glory of it! How I will revel in describing that daredevil descent to my adoring family!

Unfortunately, I have not yet paid for it, have not yet earned it.

As I climb on my bike, leave the bridge and set out once again, a bad-breathed vulture seems to settle on my shoulder. What a mistake, it observes with casual good-humored malice, to have indulged yourself with fantasies of glorious descents when you still have miles of climbing left to do. Tsk, tsk, old boy, that was a major booboo on which you will pay interest at usurious rates. See now what has happened? While you were spinning your fantasies and smugly imagining yourself resting at the bridge, age and decay have assaulted your legs.

Indeed, so they have.

When it comes to magic you can forget Braden's shy sleights of hand. "Is that the card you chose?" he asks with a hesitant bit of a grin. Time is the real magician. A magician with gravitas. When this artist saws his lovely assistant in half, he may or may not put her back together; the rabbit pulled from the top hat may hop happily off the stage, or the magician may in full view of the gasping audience eat the damn thing raw, furry and still kicking.

I don't belong on a bike, I now realize. I should be sitting beside Aunt Catherine, one in an arc of wheelchairs staring blankly at a flickering screen. I am twenty miles from home, for Christ's sake. The second summit is ten miles away and more than two thousand feet above me.

§

Steve Grogon and I took up cycling five years ago when I was sixty and Steve fifty-seven. We had met on a backpacking trip a few years earlier organized for the exchange students our families were hosting at the time. That had been my last backpacking trip. The knees and the back couldn't handle it anymore. Grogon had played tennis for years but his knees and ankles finally forced him to quit. Near the end he was popping four ibuprofens before each match and another four after.

The sprint, the springing jump shot, the sharp curve, the jarring tackle, the knife-like backhand, had all gone the way of hide 'n' seek and kick the can, casualties of impact, friction and time. But cycling seemed to be different. We started riding and we got stronger. We bought better bikes with thinner tires. We started wearing outfits wildly inappropriate for our age. We ventured farther out and came back later in the day. Flying down a hill, the reckless exuberant sense of being a child returned with a rush.

No downhill rush now; the grade is up and the thrill is gone. Over the first quarter mile a dull aching life returns to the legs but it's obvious the springs have sprung. My duty now is to find a pace, a steady spin in a low gear, each revolution of which will deliver me farther from the bridge and closer to a shower, a meal and a nap.

Musty Al, I'm thinking, pedaled through life slow and steady like this, writing poetry and noodling away on the sax. At one point he hosted a local public radio show, which, the few times I heard it, consisted mostly of Coltrane and dead air, the latter resulting from Al's abhorrence of all things technological. Had the man lived to see me now, a decade and a half older than the age at which he died, wearing this color-drenched body-tight getup, pedaling away on a bicycle through the great out-of-doors, his disdain would have been palpable. Disdain may have been Al's dominant emotion. He coated himself in it like a glossy shellac. Or, make that matte. Al did not do glossy.

The picture of Al that I'm painting for myself while true is grossly distorting. Al's disdain was toothless and offered up as a form of camaraderie. He could be quite entertaining when you got past the first encounter. His head was packed with anecdotes both personal and historical. He read constantly, observed his fellow man, his customers, his landlady, the employees in the greasy spoons and failed hotels where he took his meals. He talked with them and gossiped about them without hesitation. He saw himself and everyone around him as characters in an absurd drama that played itself out without purpose or design. Since everyone, in the end, had been assigned the role of Fool, his analysis of their behavior could seem cruel, hilarious and forgiving all at the same time. The script he recited was a lie, though, all of it. A bitter fib he told everyone, himself included.

I learned the truth of the matter when his daughter, my dear wife, betrayed everything he professed to believe in by loving him without reservation. That he finally came to accept and to trust her affection, was perhaps Al's greatest triumph. He lived to meet the infant Celeste, fell madly in love and then died, perhaps in awe of all the good that had come his way. Al's estate plan was elegant in its perfection: own nothing of value, have no one dependent on you, leave a few poems stacked in a drawer.

§

The pavement here is better than before, better in the sense that it is relatively free of potholes and hive-like patches. But it began to climb from the bridge abutment and it will continue climbing pretty much all the way to the top. Vehicles are more frequent, though frequent means one every ten minutes or so. The ascent is not as steep as the earlier climb but it goes on and on and on. Vistas now and then, bright in the sun, catch my eye but mostly I'm traveling through trees often with a high-cut bank on one side or the other. It's getting hotter; I move toward shade when I can and keep climbing.

It may be, I'm thinking, that in a perverse sort of way the love Gail gave Musty Al is what irritates her most about Braden. She sees the flow of care between me and Braden as traveling in the wrong direction, as something counter to the natural pull of gravity and time. I could have been flattered when she went on about how great a father I have been to my son, and how ungrateful he has proven himself to be. But what I felt, hearing this, was annoyance at her not-disinterested analysis. It was not true, I told myself. I had moved on with heated loins happy to leave the child in the care of his mother. Besides, what obligation did she have toward Musty Al, a man who spawned and ran off with no more a look-back than your average steelhead? Yet we took him in, turned our home over to his hospice care. It has to be that care goes where it's needed. It doesn't simply fall down through the generations like water splashing on rocks.

I do feel the need to provide something for this prodigal son of mine even knowing that what I leave him may be squandered in a rush of misplaced passion or impractical enterprise. The gambling problem hinted at by Rachel I have yet to reveal to Gail or dispassionately think through myself. Such a mess!

§

At some point while the mind is feverishly mulling all this, my body passes beyond tired and arrives at battered. Various parts and particles have begun to scream. My seat and crotch feel raw, a general ache has spread across my lower back. My thighs burn on the steeper stretches. An unwholesome transaction is taking place between a throbbing point at the base of my skull and another on my left shoulder. Then there's the damn helmet. I could swear it contains its own heat source. I want nothing more than to rip the damn thing off and toss it into the ditch.

To ease the spirit I start to count by threes from zero to the shady resting place of an even three hundred. Up and then back down, that's the practice. Picture the numbers as they pass. Think of nothing else. It's like crossing a stream on a string of carefully placed stones. Watch them appear in steady sequence. Balance yourself. "Chantele, be careful!"

Numbers have brought me a living and much comfort over the years. Awakened in the night I play only with them until they ease me gently back into sleep. Numbers are precision-engineered and self-lubricating. They possess a smooth neutrality, bring a pleasing satisfaction without stirring the passions that set the mind to whirling. You arrive at a sum, a product, and you have acquired a thing of settled value. Something you can hold in your hand or take to the bank or place on exhibit without fear of contradiction.

When it comes to age and death numbers step forward taking their place at the head of the line. That Gail will outlive me by decades is far more likely than not. That she will remarry seems reasonable, given her relative youth and vitality. Of course I would want that,

I tell myself bravely. No widow's weeds for this family! What matters any of it once I'm gone?

That on that happy day some stepfather might give Celeste away....

§

A hard swallow that one.

But it brings another thought to mind: should Gail control everything what will become of Braden? In the beginning I chose to ignore my faithful numerical friends, preferring to see Gail back then as a mature, fully developed young woman while Braden was a skinny kid just arriving at the underside of puberty. To see, in other words, only with my yearning heart: to imagine that Gail and Braden came from different generations while she and I shared the same. It was a comfortable though unsustainable illusion. When Gail has reached her dotage at eighty-five, Braden will have passed seventy and still be waiting off stage like some unanointed Prince Charles. If he has to await her death will he get anything at all, he being of the early-dying gender? Or will there be anything left to give, she having spent it all? Or, might she not at some future date, she now remarried and me but a distant memory, alter whatever plans we so carefully prepare, cutting Braden out entirely for one easily imagined reason or another?

On the other hand, were I to insist on a generous gift to Braden at my death, which he then squanders in a few months, and my dear Gail lives on for another quarter century or more with less than she needs to be comfortable…. Or, heaven forbid, something happens to Celeste that requires our help…. I remember well the inflation of the late seventies and the string of bubbles that have blossomed and popped in the years since.

It was Musty Al and his death-engorged pancreas that first brought home the hard numbers that separate me from Gail. The maturity that I had gloried in, that I liked to imagine helped lure the lovely young French teacher to my side, was now a gulf opening between us. I was the same age as this gray and puffy, soon-to-be-dead man we lifted from his stacks of curling paperbacks and faded album covers, hauled to California and loaded into the spare bedroom. Surely, Gail, with her Gallic-honed instincts, is as aware of this fact as I. Perhaps she saw the care she gave to Al as practice for the care she would eventually bring to me. I certainly did. And I realized as I watched her carry out this noble work that a sense of profound loyalty runs through my wife's character. It is a pillar, central, strong, structural. Never have I felt such tenderness and love for her as when I watched her ministering to Al. Relief as well. I too would one day be so sheltered, looked after, fussed over, ministered to, hand-delivered to the final doorway.

§

The counting trick does not work. Each time I start the journey from three to three hundred the mind strays back to family, to distance and pain.

The immediate goal is a junction six miles from the bridge. The road to the right will lead to the summit and from there I will begin the much-anticipated ten-mile descent toward home. As I near the junction the pavement makes a hairpin turn as if it were scurrying back and forth along the flank of the hill, searching for an opening where it could turn up and climb to the top. The slant of the hill has become extraordinarily pronounced, and the road, set on a narrow shelf cut into the hill's side, seems to shrink back from the edge.

The rate of climb had been gentler for a while but now it becomes steeper again and I am out of breath and badly in need of a break when I finally see a sign that the junction lies ahead. Then the road itself appears, cutting up and sharply back like the barb on a fishhook.

My God, I realize when I stop, it's gravel. I had forgotten that the next two miles are gravel.

6

I set my bike in the grass and walk slowly back and forth along the edge of the road. I have no wish to sit, or rest, or even stop moving. It feels best to pace. My mouth is dry and the warm water I swallow does little to change that. The remains of the energy bar that I force down bears an unpleasant resemblance to cardboard laced with peanut butter.

Gail and Celeste enter my mind with an explosion of color. I imagine them sitting at an outdoor table somewhere in the city, looking leggy and chic in their sunglasses, ice tea for mom, lemonade for daughter, a few bright shopping bags tilting at their feet, the two of them giggling over the menu. A sense of youth dominates the sunny picture basking in my mind's eye. So young! A casual observer might mistake the two of them for sisters.

But then the picture darkens as I pace and other thoughts come to mind. I had assumed we were both going to pick up Celeste. But then on Tuesday morning, the morning after the seminar, Gail had suggested she go alone.

"The trunk will be packed to the top, you know that. And we'll need every square inch of the backseat just to fit everything in."

I said, "Well we took her down together last fall. It was cramped, but we made it."

"You know how Celeste is, hon. Trust me, she's been accumulating stuff all year long. Enjoy the weekend. Ride your bike."

"It's Mother's Day weekend."

"I know, and that's great, but we can celebrate together that evening. The three of us, when we get back."

I felt released, to tell the truth. It left me free to try the Loop. I sent off my first email to Steve Grogon later that morning.

But what if I had it all wrong? I think now. What if Gail's eagerness to get us into Mr. Slick-Suit's seminar had been prompted more by concern for her own pending demise than my own? Musty Al's young death from cancer lodged a qualm in her psyche that has never gone away. Then a few years later a pre-cancerous abnormality showed up on a Pap smear that resulted in a cervical "scraping" at a gynecological clinic. Since then every exam has been normal. But have I been missing something? Did she have things to talk about that she has not brought to me because of my annoyance at her morose moods, my irritation with her urgent need for an estate plan? Have I been acting old and cantankerous, pushing her away? Is she more comfortable now revealing her deepest fears to Celeste than to me?

With a sudden nervous clutch I grope for my cell phone. I pull it from the pouch, turn it on and find I have no signal.

A shy touch of breeze seems to press against the hot air but then stops as if the effort were too much. In the tan-dirt ditch beside the road a strewing of beer cans and the weathered-wrapping from a discarded twelve-pack. From the dense underbrush on the uphill side comes an occasional discrete sound: a junco flutters its wings, a branch cracks, a living creature is snapped up and devoured.

Your thinking has become deranged, I tell myself. Get on the damn bike and pedal your butt home.

§

The gravel stretch proves steep, treacherous, washboardy, exhausting. I travel in my lowest gear moving along at three and a half miles an hour with all the vigor of a banana slug. I check and recheck the odometer with manic compulsion, trying to calculate the exact distance between my location and the top. My faithful numbers have been wrenched from their neutrality and set to spinning in my mind.

By the time I reach the narrow strip of pavement and begin the final steep ascent, my surroundings have become withdrawn, shadow-like. I feel my consciousness descend into a dim hypnotic-like trance that I know to be dangerous.

I hear then a vehicle rattling and banging along the gravel road behind me. As it approaches, the compounding racket seems to signify everything loud and aggressive and oblivious about the species to which we belong. The vehicle arrives at the pavement and accelerates even more. I'm too unstable to share the road with this roaring machine. Just before it reaches me I pull off into the trees. But putting my foot to the ground, my shoe fails to unlock from the pedal-clip and I fall sideways into a tangle of huckleberry and weeds. I'm lying in the mangled bush with the bike still between my legs, my feet locked securely to the pedals, a position best described as impossible.

The vehicle stops. A door slams. I'm frantically kicking to free my feet when I see before my eyes a pair of battered cowboy boots. Standing in them is a tall, big-boned woman with a large head covered with reddish-brown hair beginning to gray. She wears leather gloves, jeans and a work shirt. The paunch emerging below the western belt buckle is particularly prominent from my perspective. It is, I realize, the alfalfa-pitching bull owner I had passed much earlier in the day.

"You all right?" she asks, a grin spreading across her wide and burnished face.

"I'm fine, damnit." I finally wrest my right foot free. "Here, hold the bike will you?"

She grabs hold.

"No! Don't lift it. Just hold it there."

"Right." The grin becomes even more pronounced.

I pull my other foot free, stagger from the bush and take the bike out of her hands.

"That was quite a landing," she observes.

"Foot caught."

"I see that. Thought at first you'd just keeled over dead. End of the trail sort of thing."

"Well, I'm not dead, damnit."

"I see that too," the woman says. "You wouldn't be bleeding like that if you was dead." She points down at my left leg.

"Shit." An abrasion runs along my shin and a stream of blood is flowing onto my sock. I push the bike back into her hands and bend down to examine the leg. "It's just a scrape," I tell her. "It'll stop."

"Reckon it will," she agrees, "sooner or later. Meanwhile you want a lift to town? We could toss that bike in the bed of the truck. Have you there in fifteen-twenty minutes."

I take the bike back and run a quick check. The wheels turn freely. The brakes and drive train seem fine. I push the bike to the edge of the road and study the strip of asphalt climbing up through the trees.

"I want to finish."

"Are you sure?" asks the bull owner.

Gail does that at times. She asks a question and then when I've given my answer, she asks if I really meant what I just said. As if my decisions were like ice cream; that they begin to melt as soon as they see the light of day.

"You think maybe I'm not sure?" I ask with what I suspect is a cold glare. "You think maybe I'm a little confused or something?"

"No, I..."

"Well, I am sure. I want to finish the ride."

"Fine."

"And tomorrow I'm going to call Dave Silver too. First thing...."

The woman is staring at me.

"That's fine," she says again. "I'll be on my way then." She starts moving toward her truck.

"Look, I'm...."

"No, really, it's fine."

A moment later the door of the truck slams shut and she is gone, leaving behind a cloud of noise and exhaust fumes and the fading scent of alfalfa.

I lean the bike against a tree and examine it again. Both water bottles have fallen out. I walk to the scene of the crash, find the bottles and drink much of what remains in the second bottle. It is very quiet. I sit down in the duff and lean back against the narrow trunk of a tanoak.

The still, sun-dappled air smells of heated vegetation. Everything at this moment possesses a strange beauty. It appears to me extraordinarily bright and glistening, as if I were looking at the world through a thin film of water. Don't be an idiot, I tell myself. You're not crying. You're just exhausted. You have lots of time. There are hours of daylight left and they won't be home until late. Sit here a moment and you'll be good as new. I take my helmet off and lean my damp head against the tree. The blood has begun to clot. I can feel it tightening as it dries along my shin.

Musty Al is watching me from a few feet away. I can see him quite clearly. He's slowly shaking his head and not bothering to suppress a grin. Al knows exactly who I am; you can almost see the story forming in the man's head. He will chuckle and smirk as he tells my tale to anyone who cares to listen.

FRAGMENT

Item 39. Participant, having chosen to enroll in the immersion program entitled One Physical Life—Earth—Human (see Item 3 above with accompanying notes and illustrations), does hereby acknowledge that during the course of said immersion, participant will confuse role with self, forget origin and the making of this agreement, and will from time-to-time experience Existential Dread i.e., fear of nonexistence. The sensation will be particularly pronounced in relation to Exiting the Program. (Exiting the Program is described in detail below beginning with Item 40.)